SHELBY & WATTS

Tide Pool Troubles

by ashlyn anstee

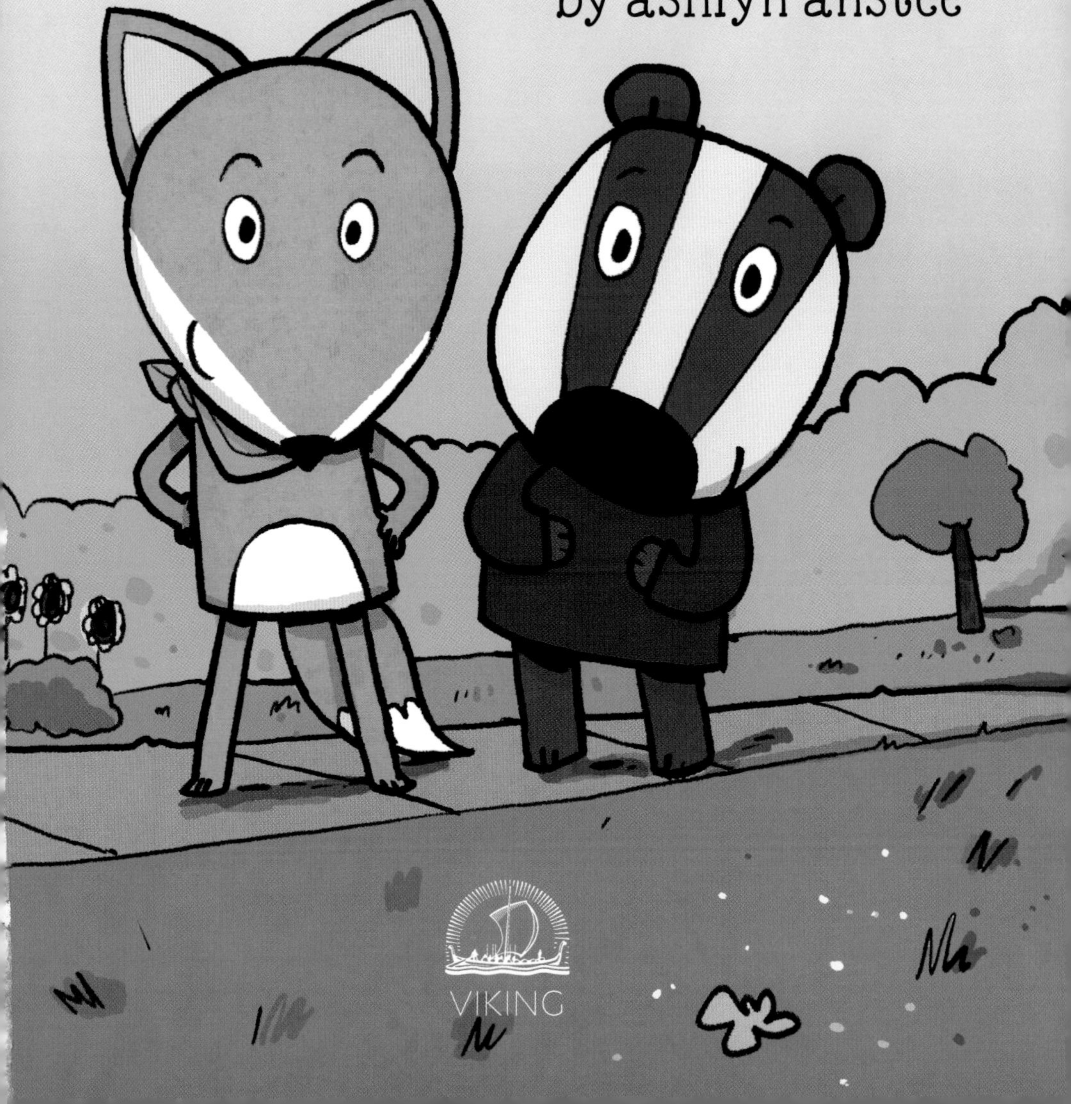

VIKING

CHAPTER 1

In the village of Valley Glen . . .

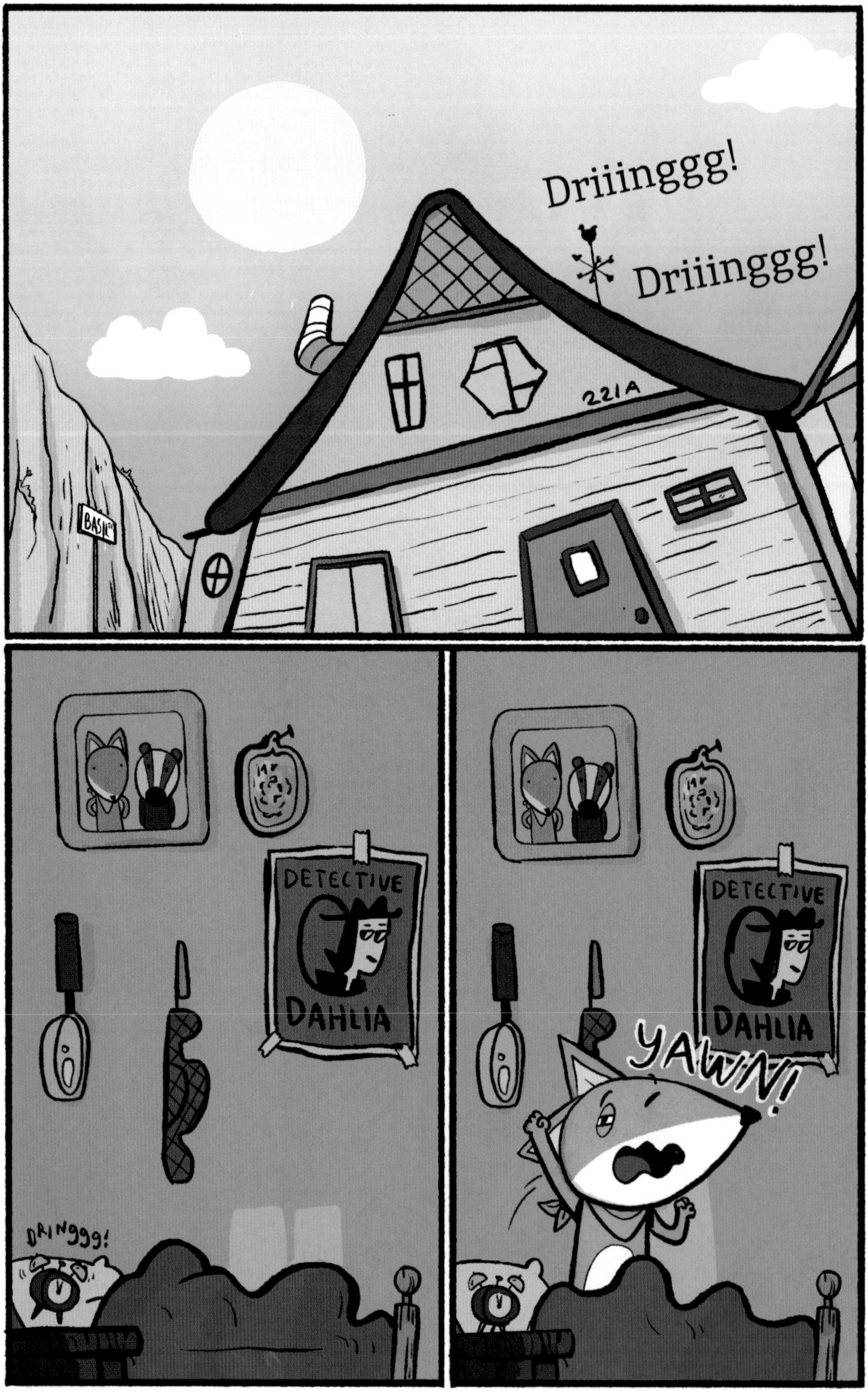
Driiinggg!
Driiinggg!
221A
BASIL ST
DETECTIVE DAHLIA
DRINggg!
DETECTIVE DAHLIA
YAWN!

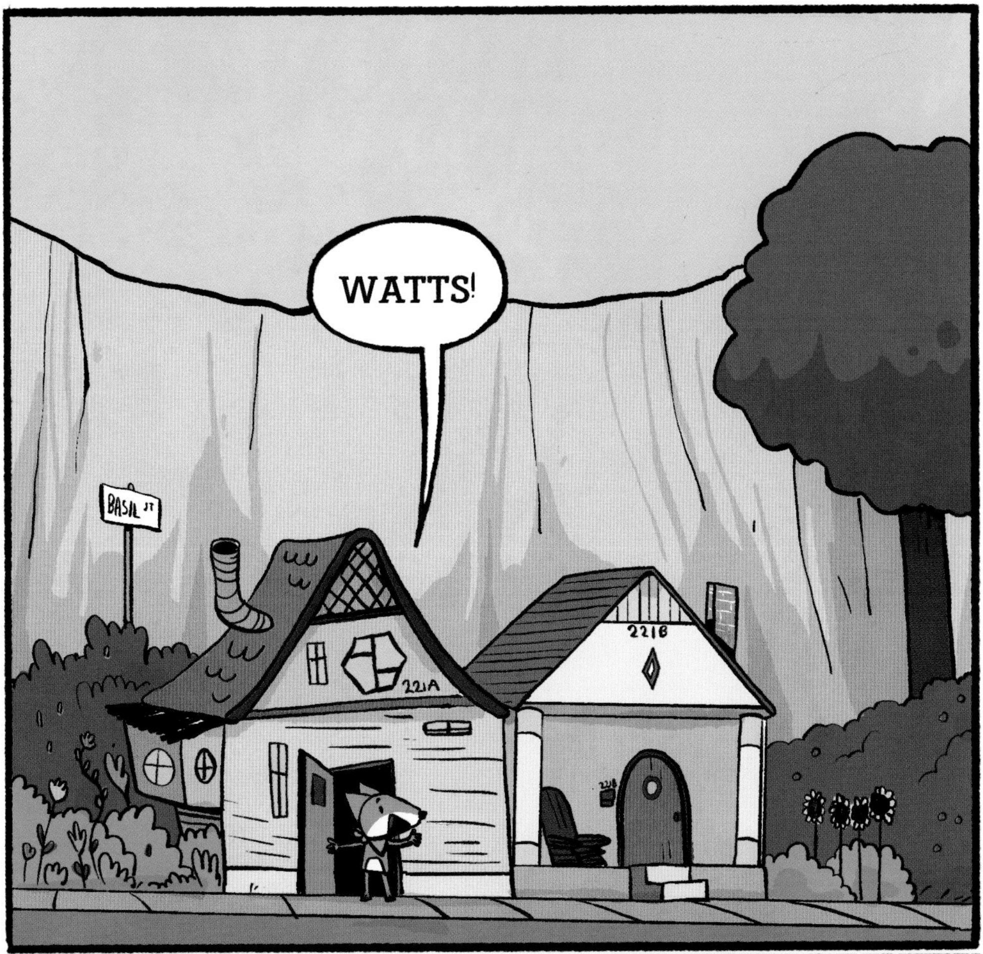
WATTS!
BASIL ST
221A
221B

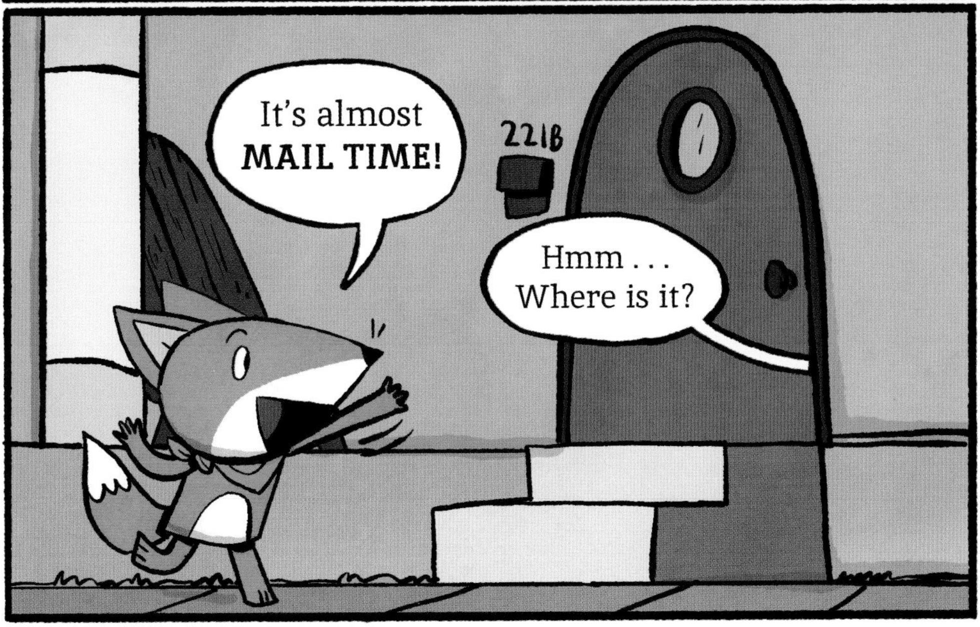
It's almost **MAIL TIME!**
221B
Hmm . . .
Where is it?

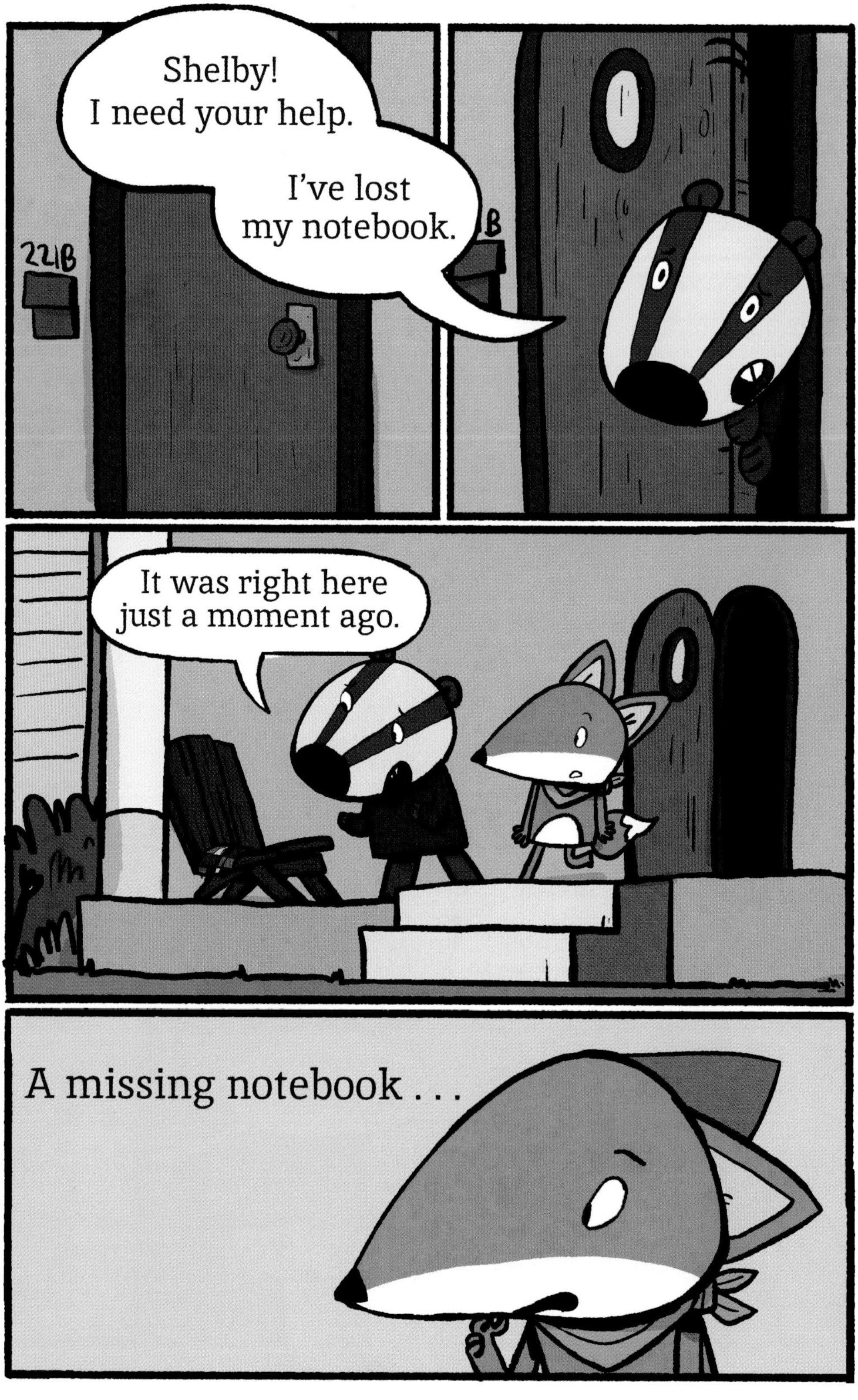
221B
Shelby! I need your help.
I've lost my notebook.
It was right here just a moment ago.
A missing notebook . . .

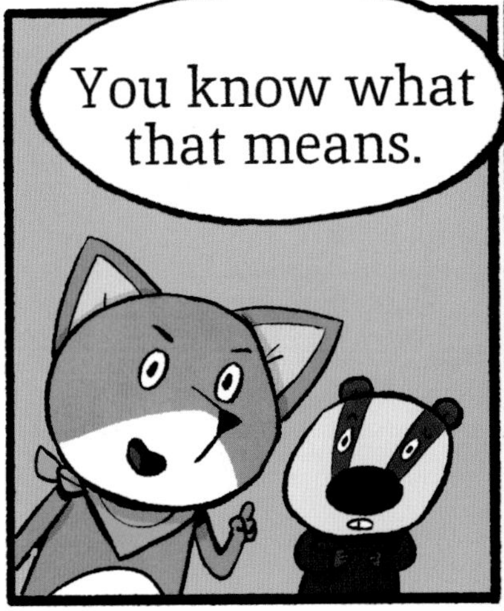
You know what that means.

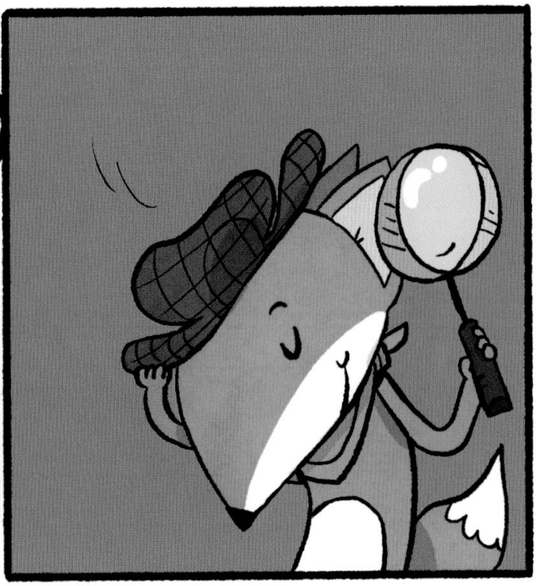

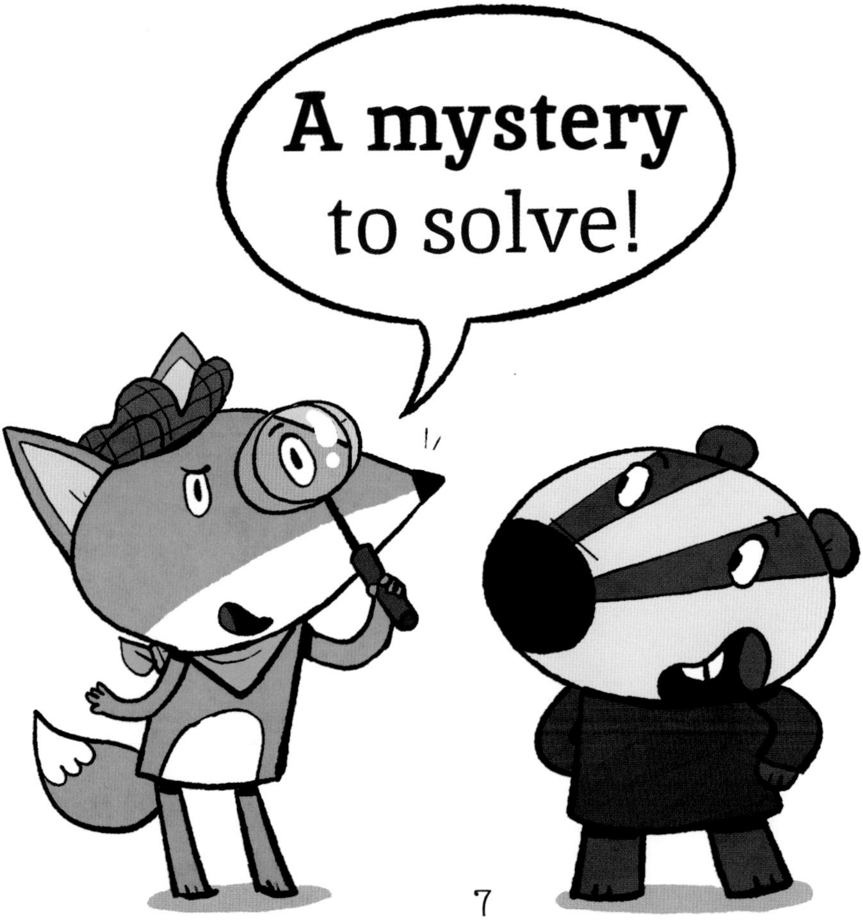
A mystery to solve!

Shelby

fox

favorite book:
*Detective Dahlia
and the Sounds of Basketville*
favorite color: teal

Watts

badger

favorite book:
Encyclopedia of the World
(unabridged), 5th Edition
favorite color: maroon

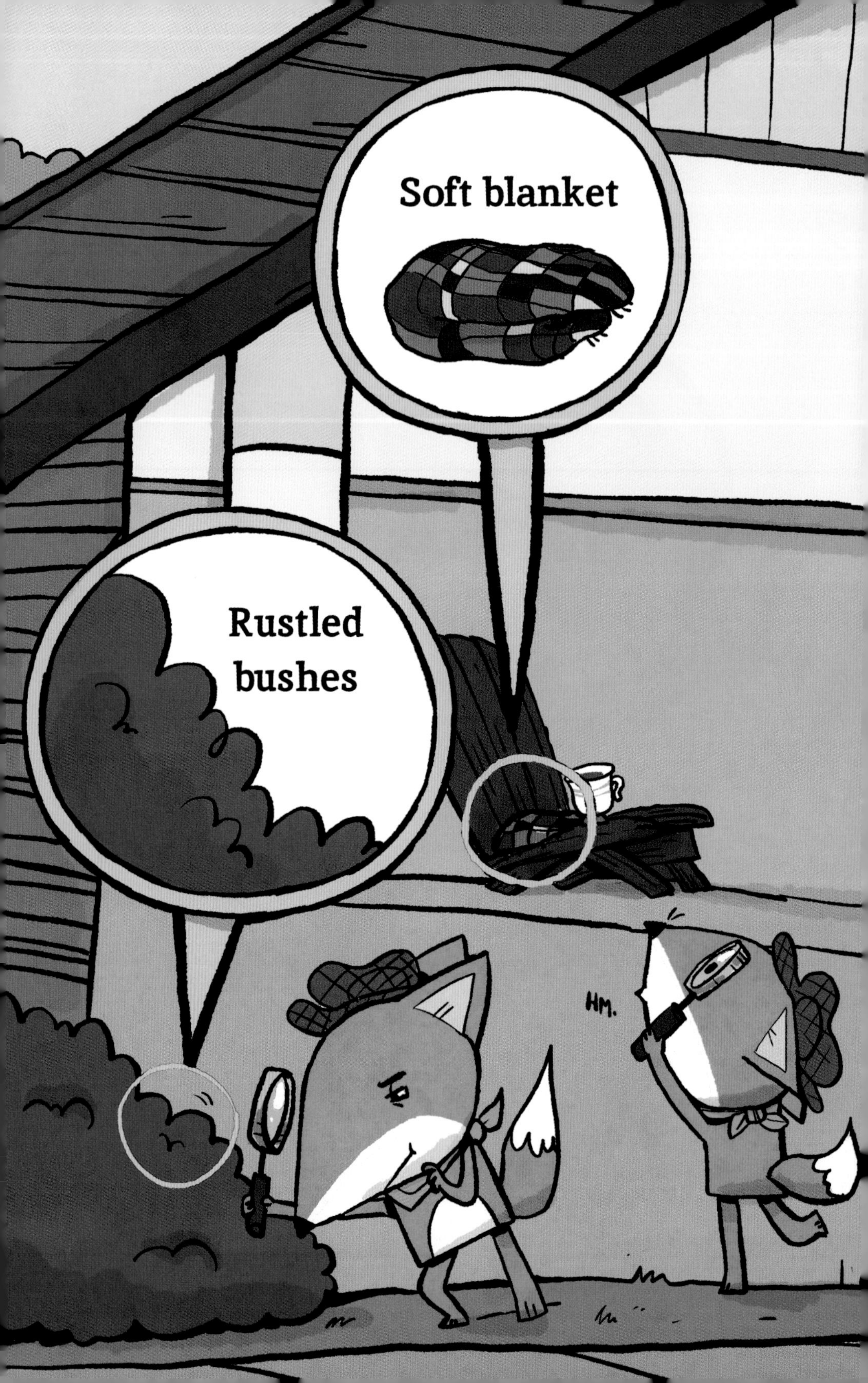
Soft blanket
Rustled bushes
HM.

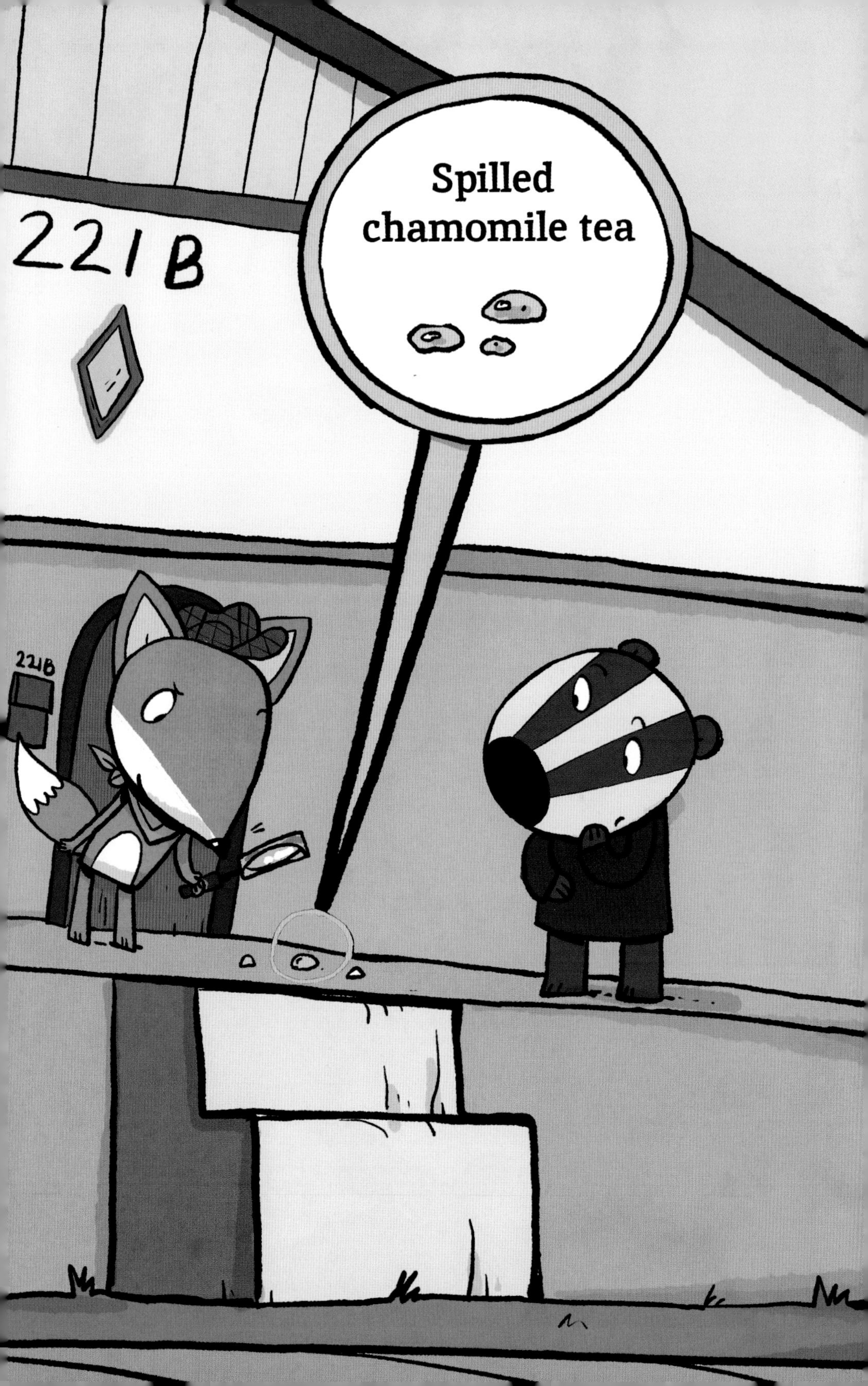
221B
Spilled chamomile tea
221B

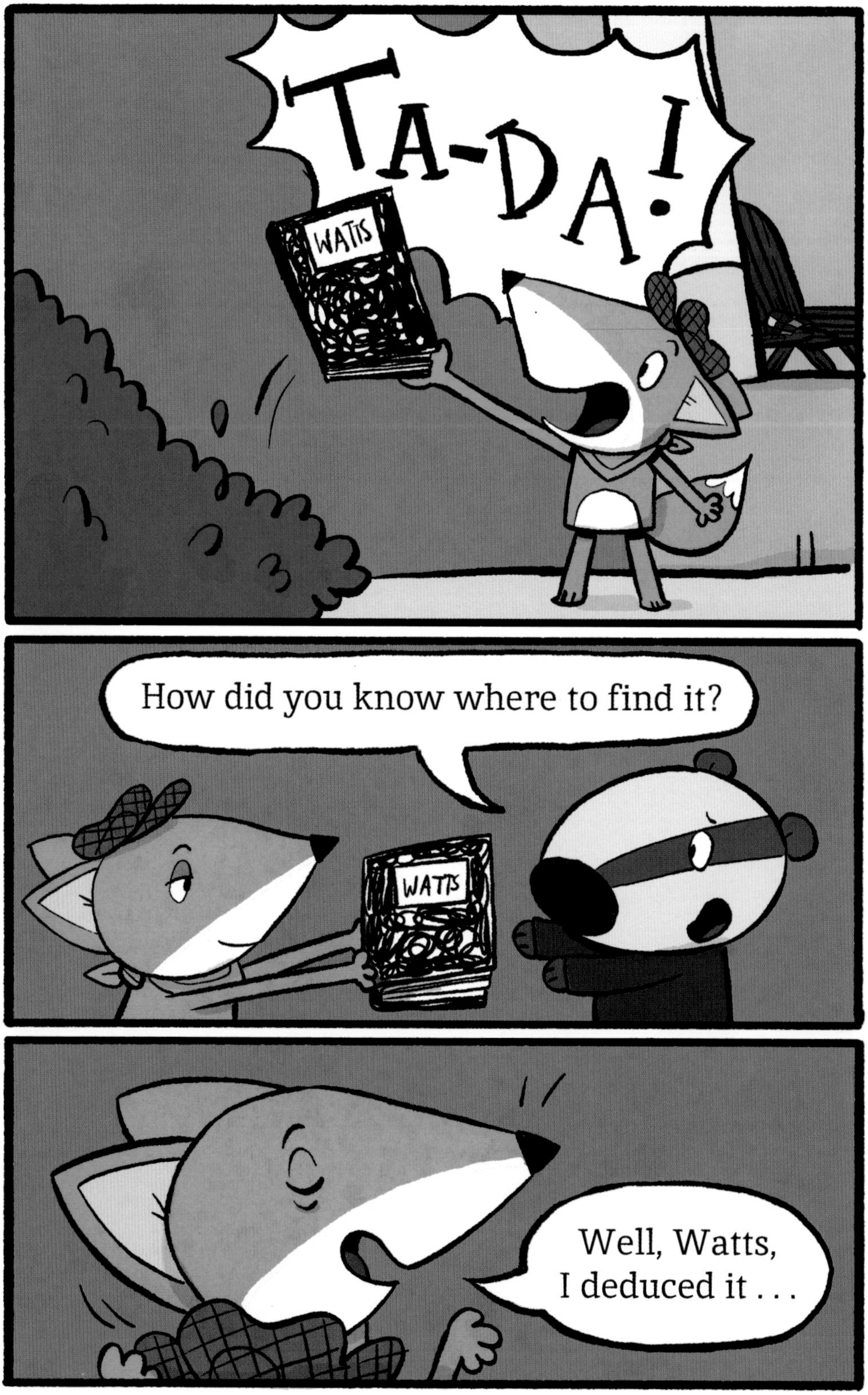
TA-DA!
WATTS
How did you know where to find it?
WATTS
Well, Watts,
I deduced it . . .

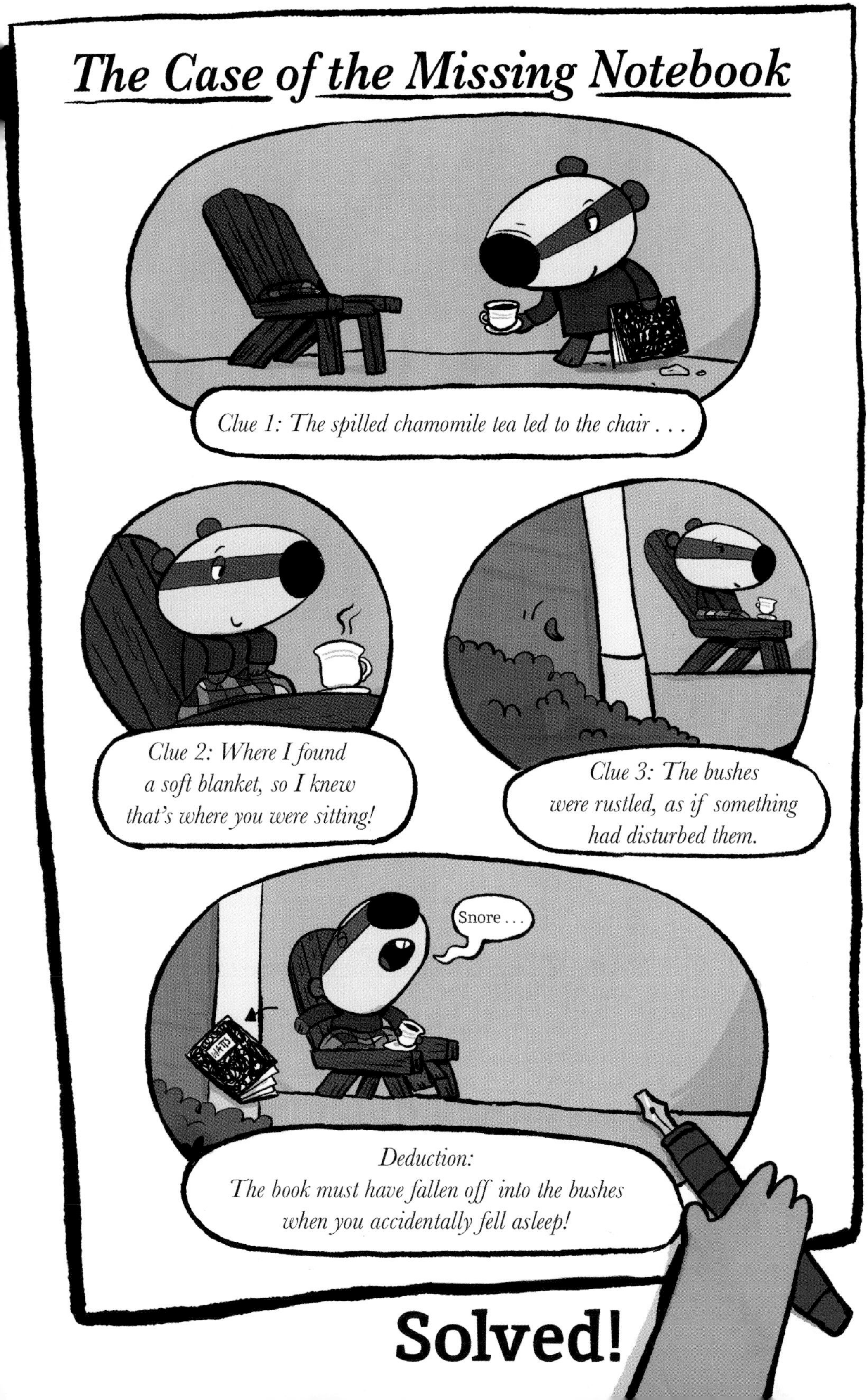
The Case of the Missing Notebook
Clue 1: The spilled chamomile tea led to the chair . . .
Clue 2: Where I found a soft blanket, so I knew that's where you were sitting!
Clue 3: The bushes were rustled, as if something had disturbed them.
Snore . . .
Deduction: The book must have fallen off into the bushes when you accidentally fell asleep!
Solved!

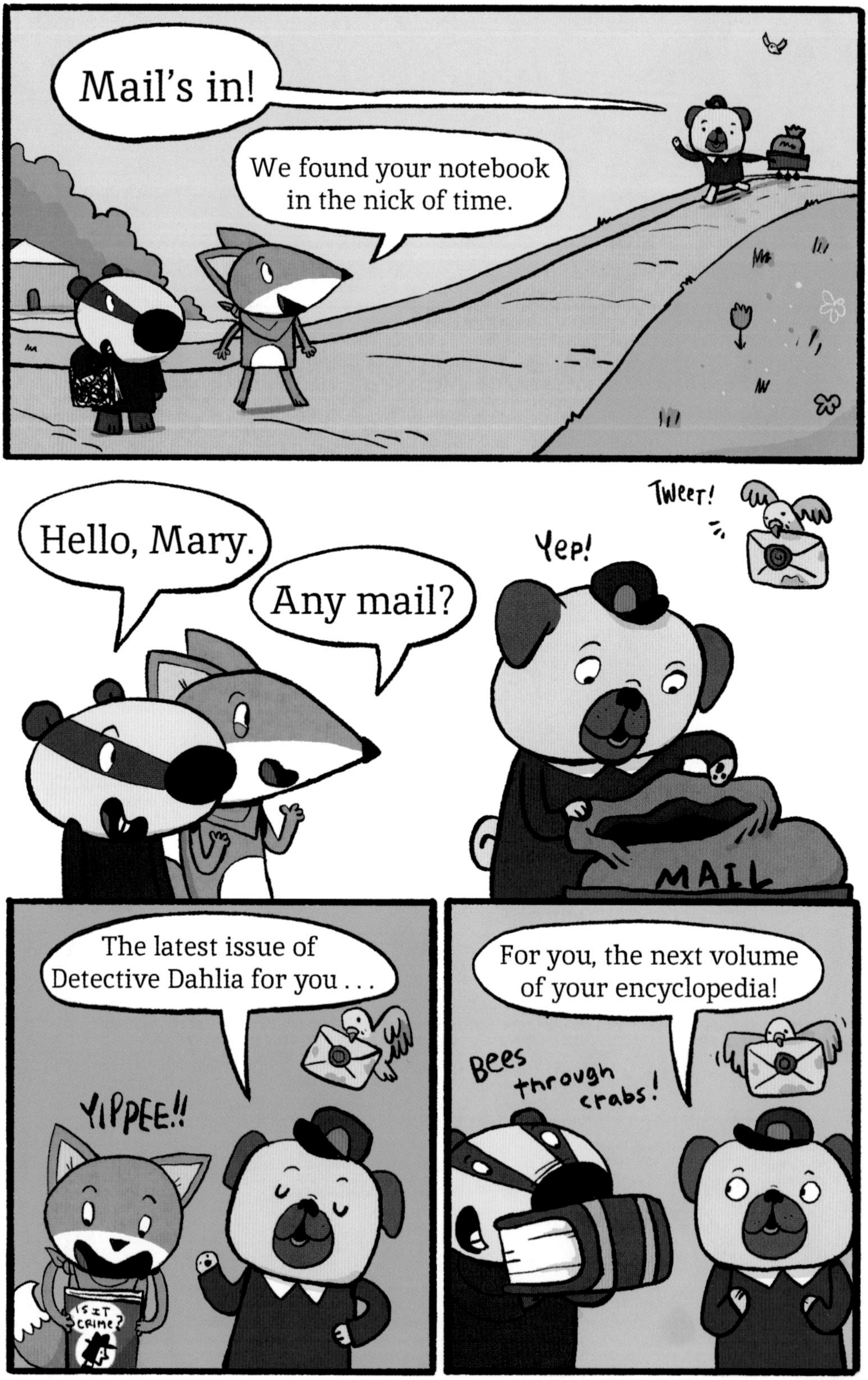
Mail's in!
We found your notebook in the nick of time.
Hello, Mary.
Any mail?
Yep!
TWEET!
MAIL
The latest issue of Detective Dahlia for you . . .
YIPPEE!!
IS IT CRIME?
For you, the next volume of your encyclopedia!
Bees through crabs!

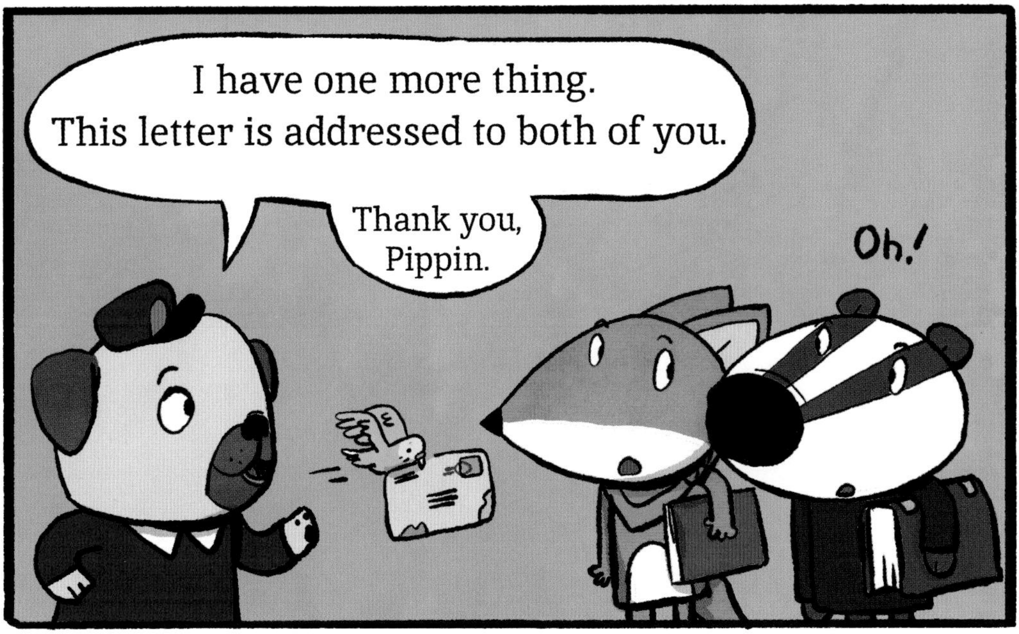
I have one more thing.
This letter is addressed to both of you.
Thank you, Pippin.
Oh!

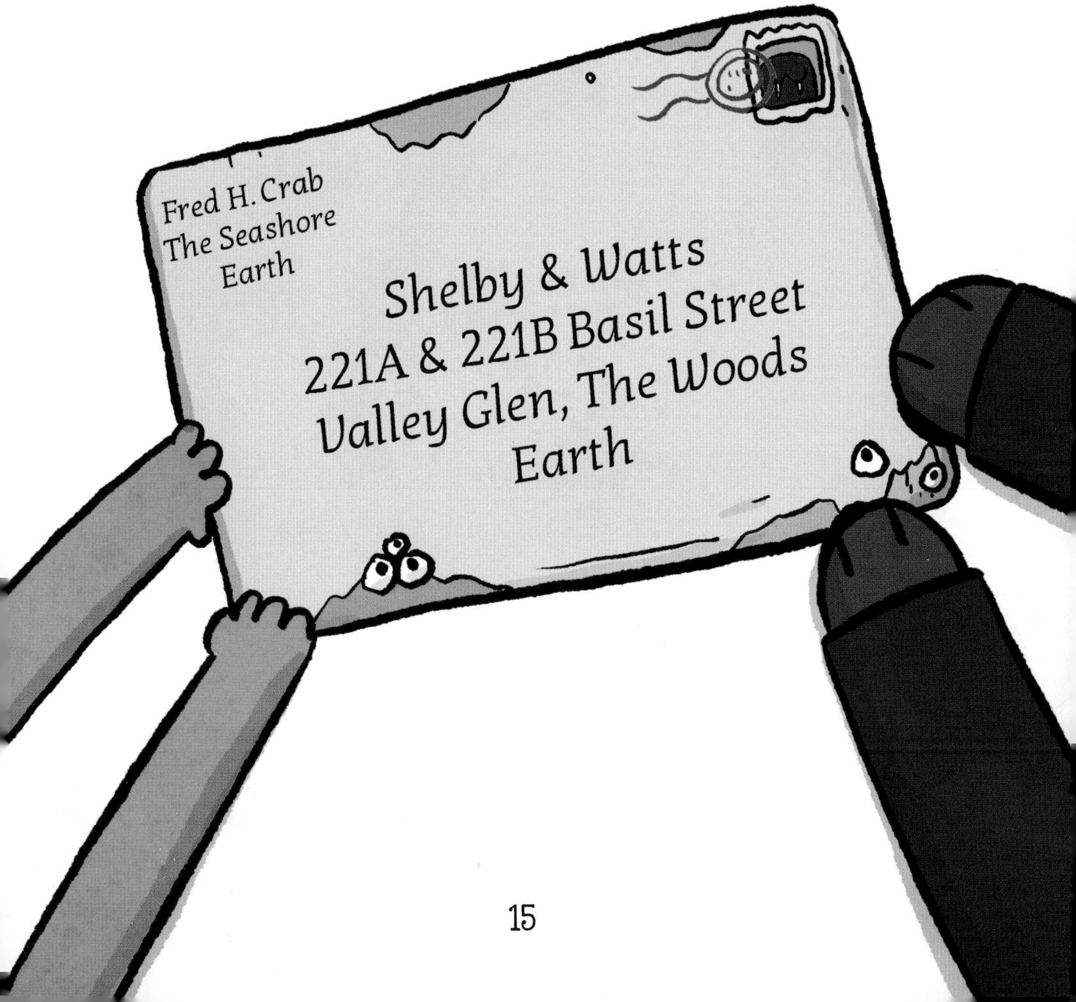
Fred H. Crab
The Seashore
Earth
Shelby & Watts
221A & 221B Basil Street
Valley Glen, The Woods
Earth

Dear Shelby and Watts,

I'm sorry for writing you out of the blue, but I need your help.

My name is Fred and I'm a hermit crab.

My shell has become too small and I can't find a big enough shell to move into.

There isn't one ANYWHERE on the beach!

Shelby—Mary told me that you've read more mysteries than anyone she knows.

Watts—Mary said that you've read the whole encyclopedia cover to cover.

This is a mystery that needs both of your brilliant brains.

So please, would you help me find a new shell?

I'm in quite a pickle.

Anxiously awaiting your visiting,

FRED

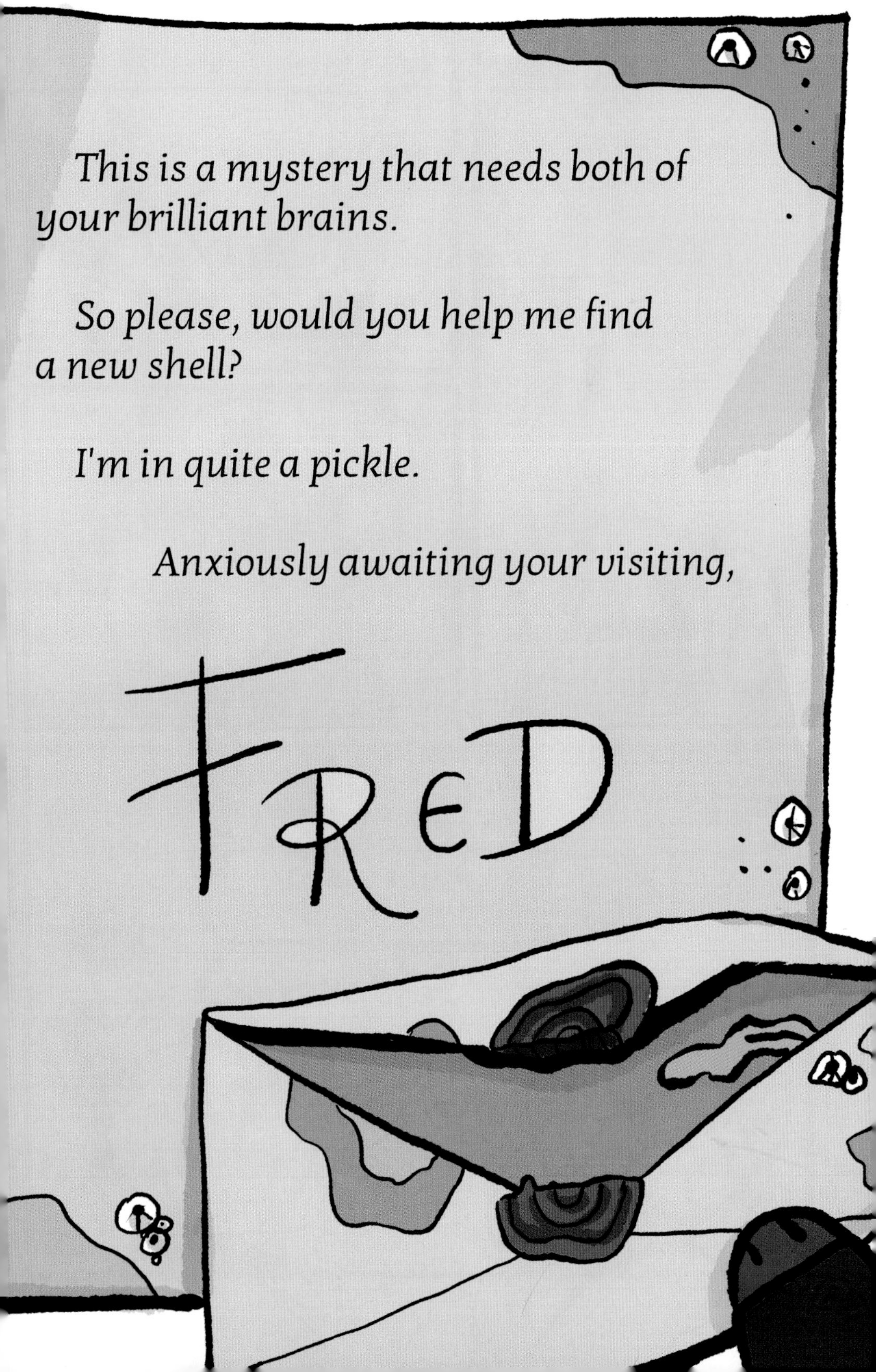

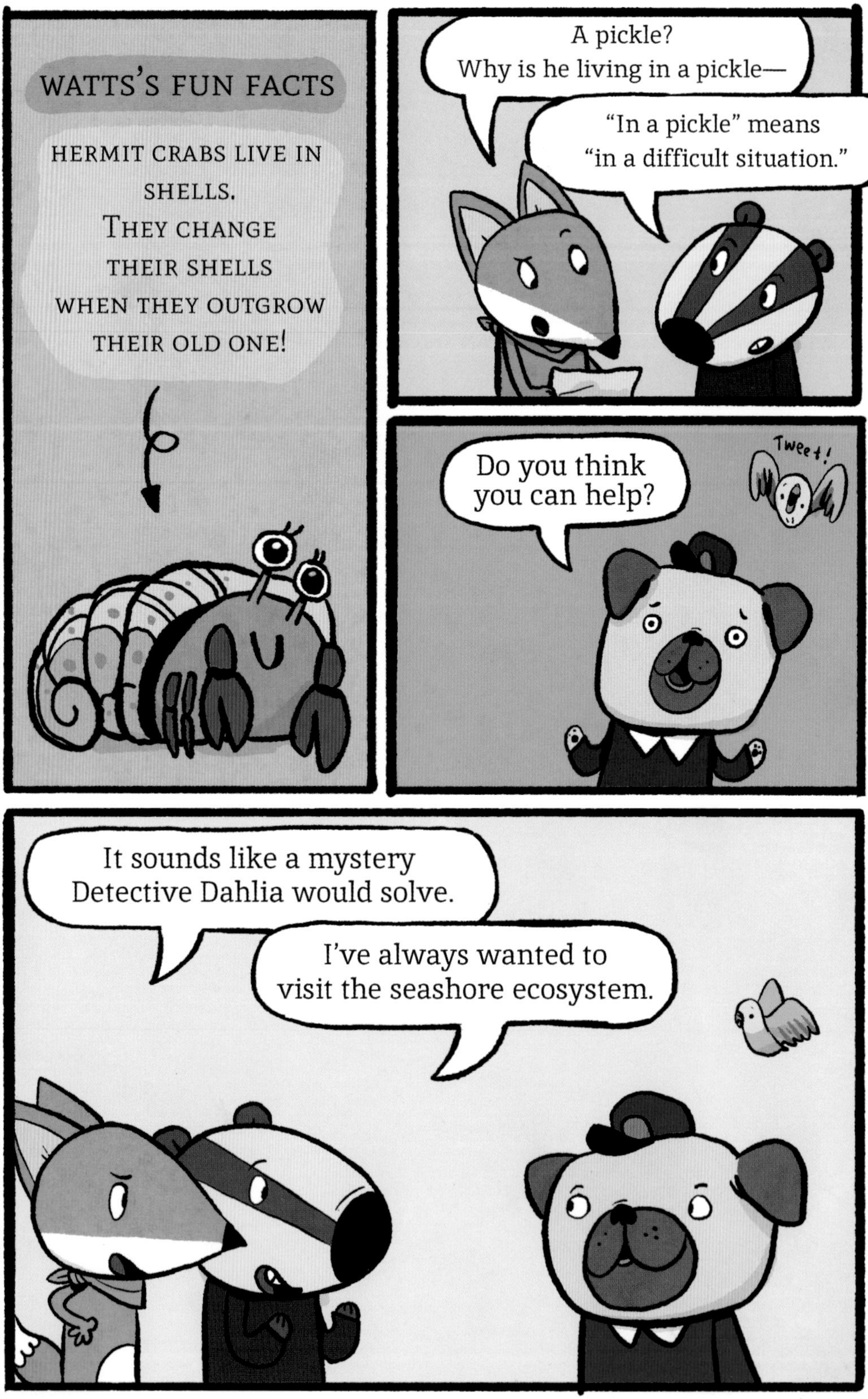
WATTS'S FUN FACTS
HERMIT CRABS LIVE IN SHELLS. THEY CHANGE THEIR SHELLS WHEN THEY OUTGROW THEIR OLD ONE!
A pickle? Why is he living in a pickle—
"In a pickle" means "in a difficult situation."
Do you think you can help?
Tweet!
It sounds like a mystery Detective Dahlia would solve.
I've always wanted to visit the seashore ecosystem.

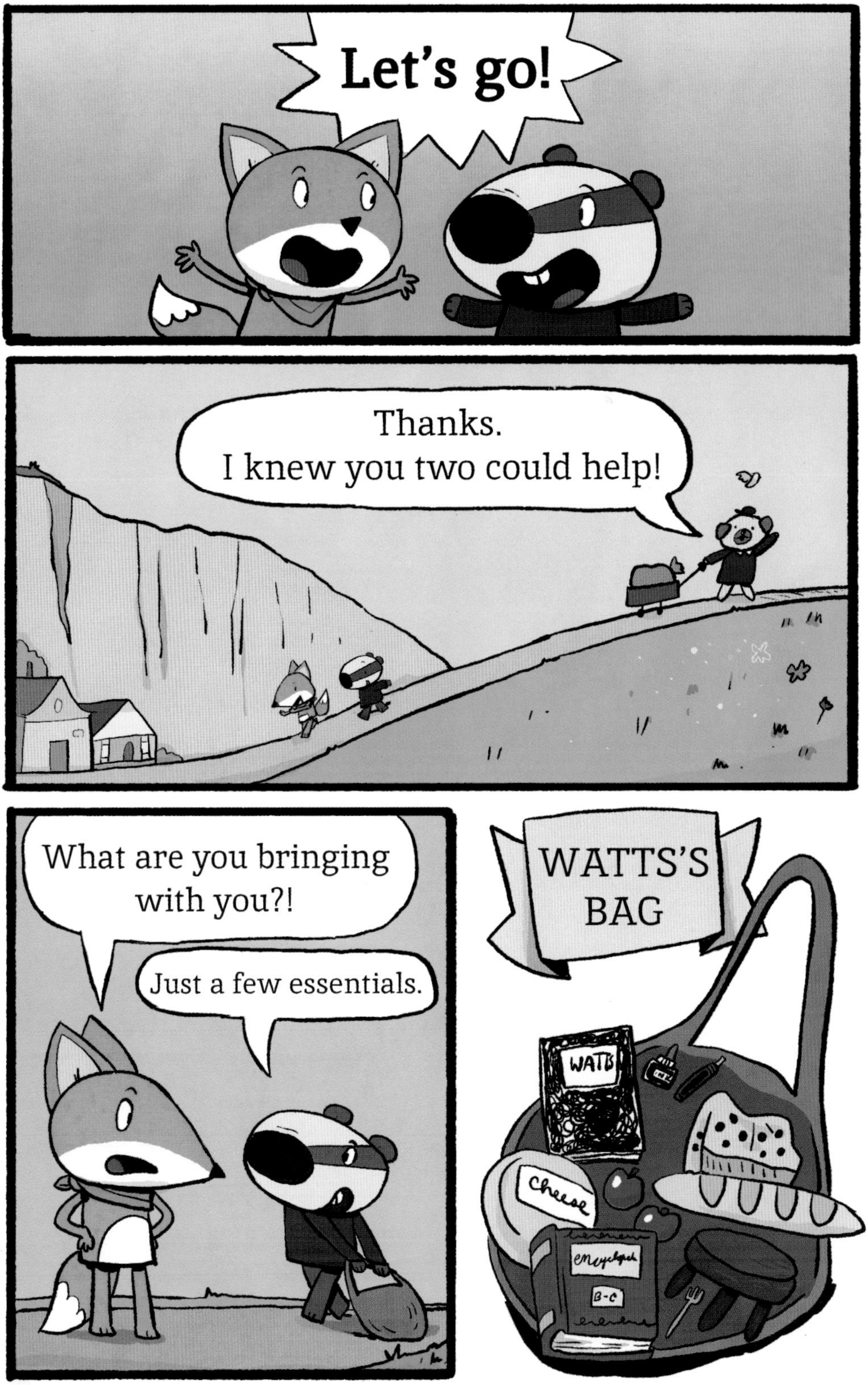
Let's go!
Thanks.
I knew you two could help!
What are you bringing with you?!
Just a few essentials.
WATTS'S BAG
WATTS
Cheese
B-C

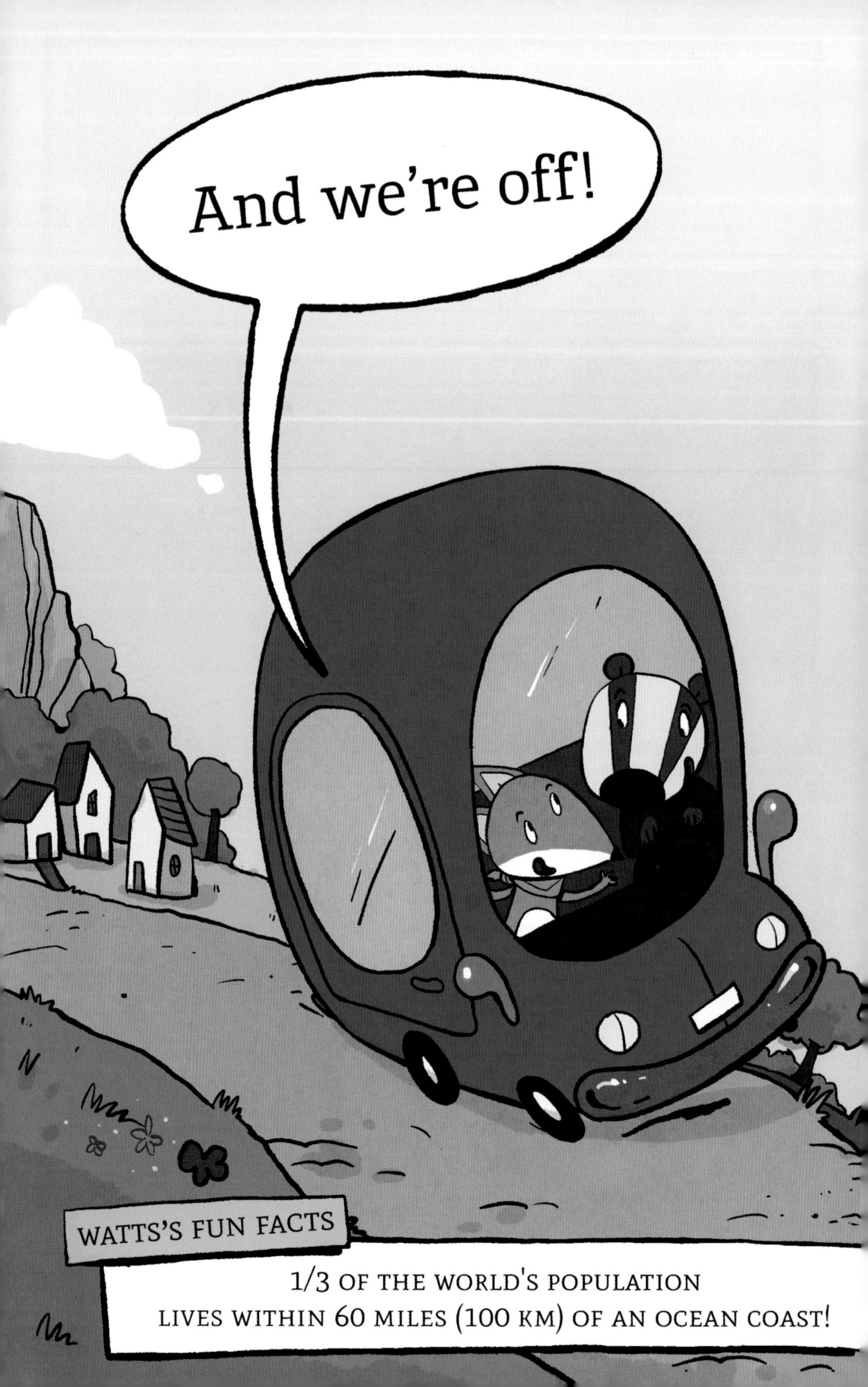
And we're off!

WATTS'S FUN FACTS

1/3 OF THE WORLD'S POPULATION LIVES WITHIN 60 MILES (100 KM) OF AN OCEAN COAST!

CHAPTER 2

At the beach dunes . . .

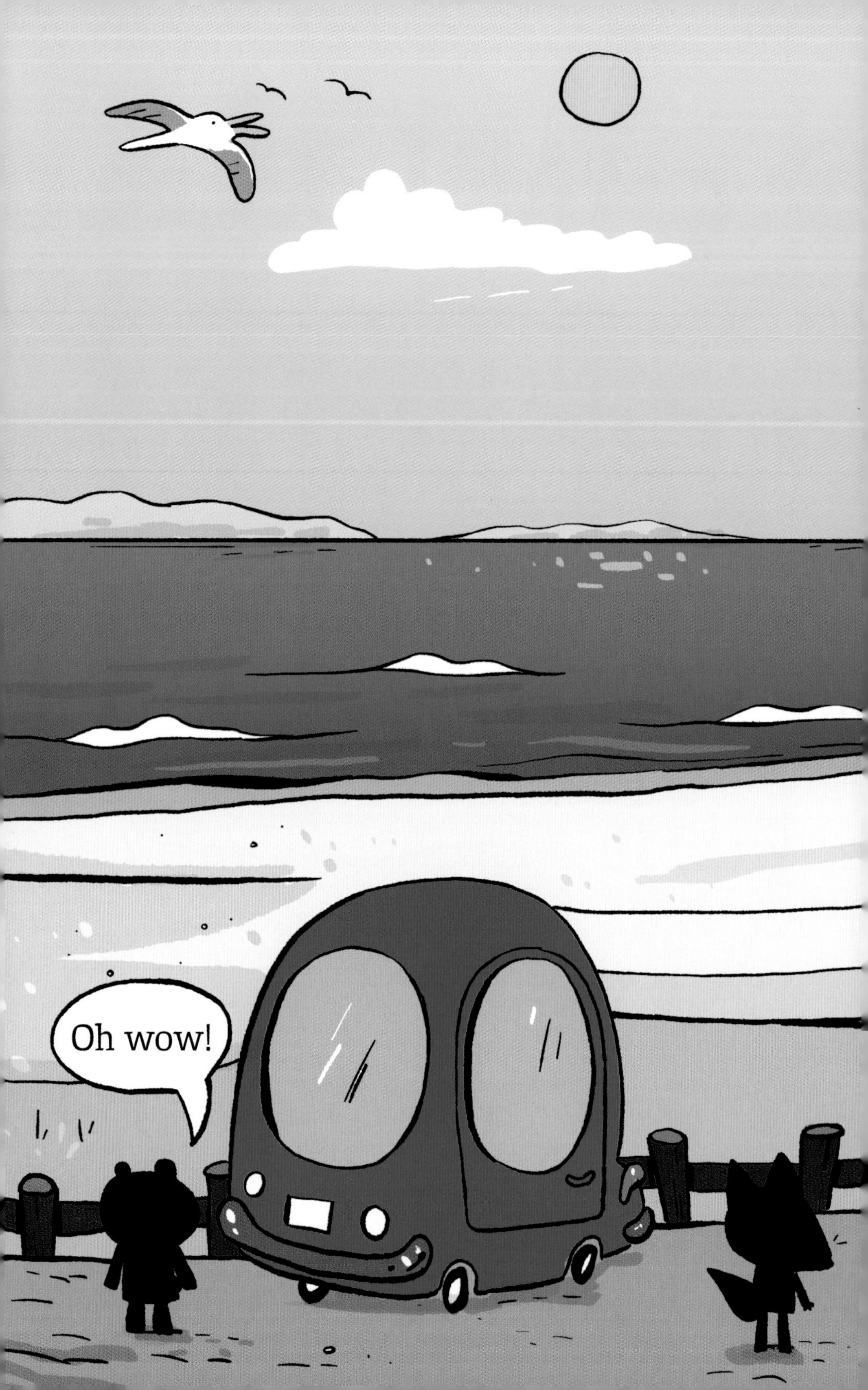
Oh wow!

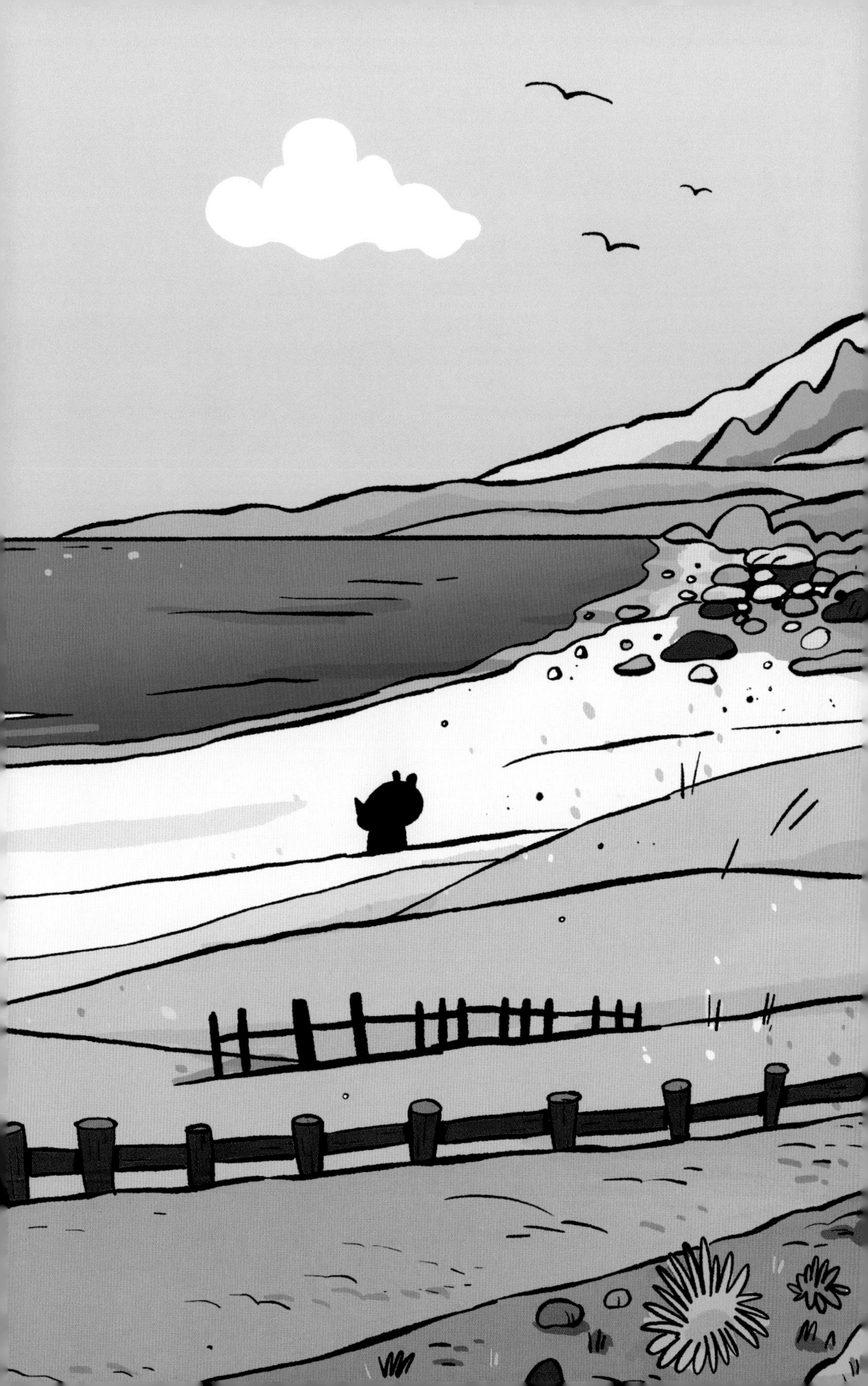

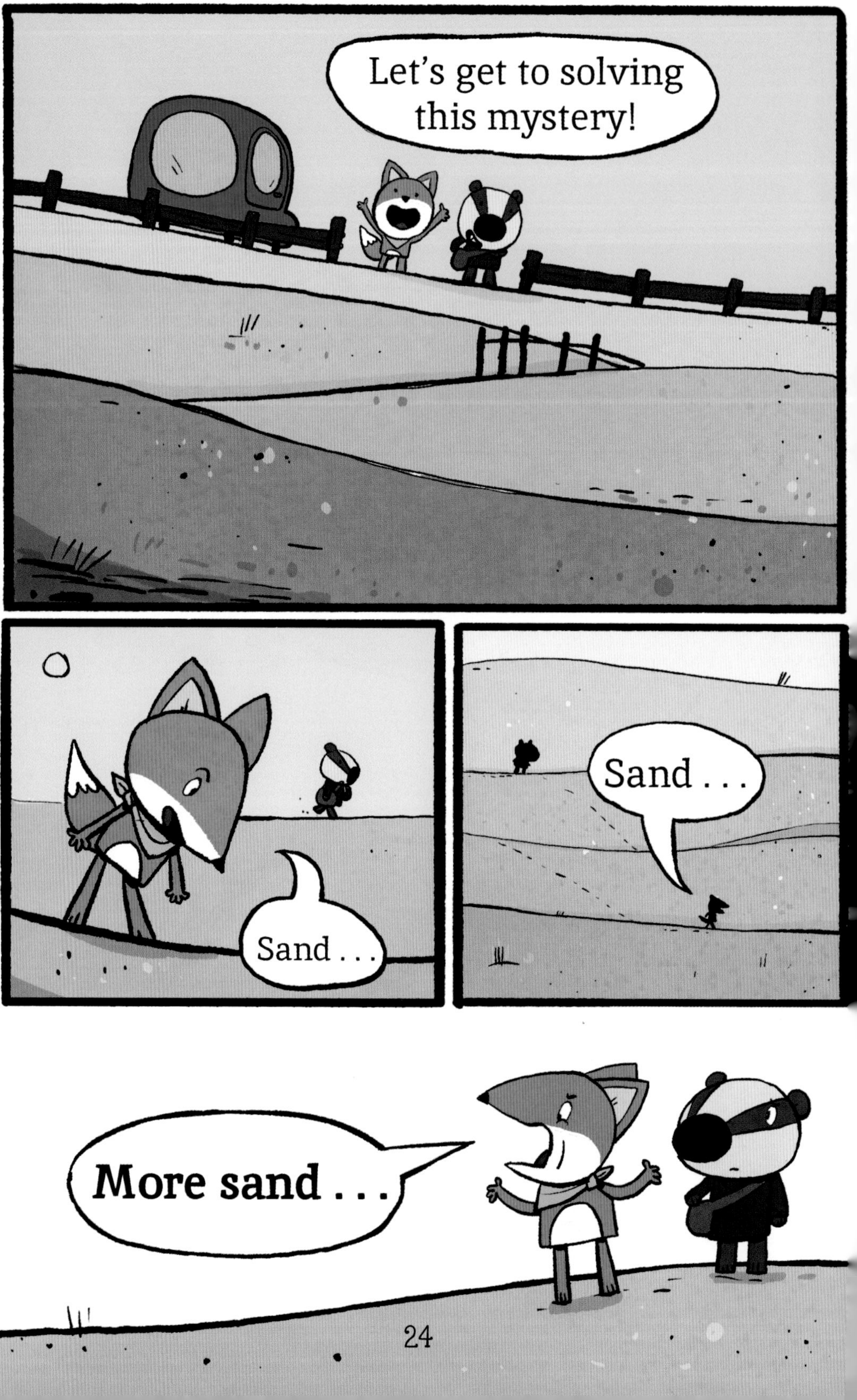
Let's get to solving this mystery!
Sand . . .
Sand . . .
More sand . . .

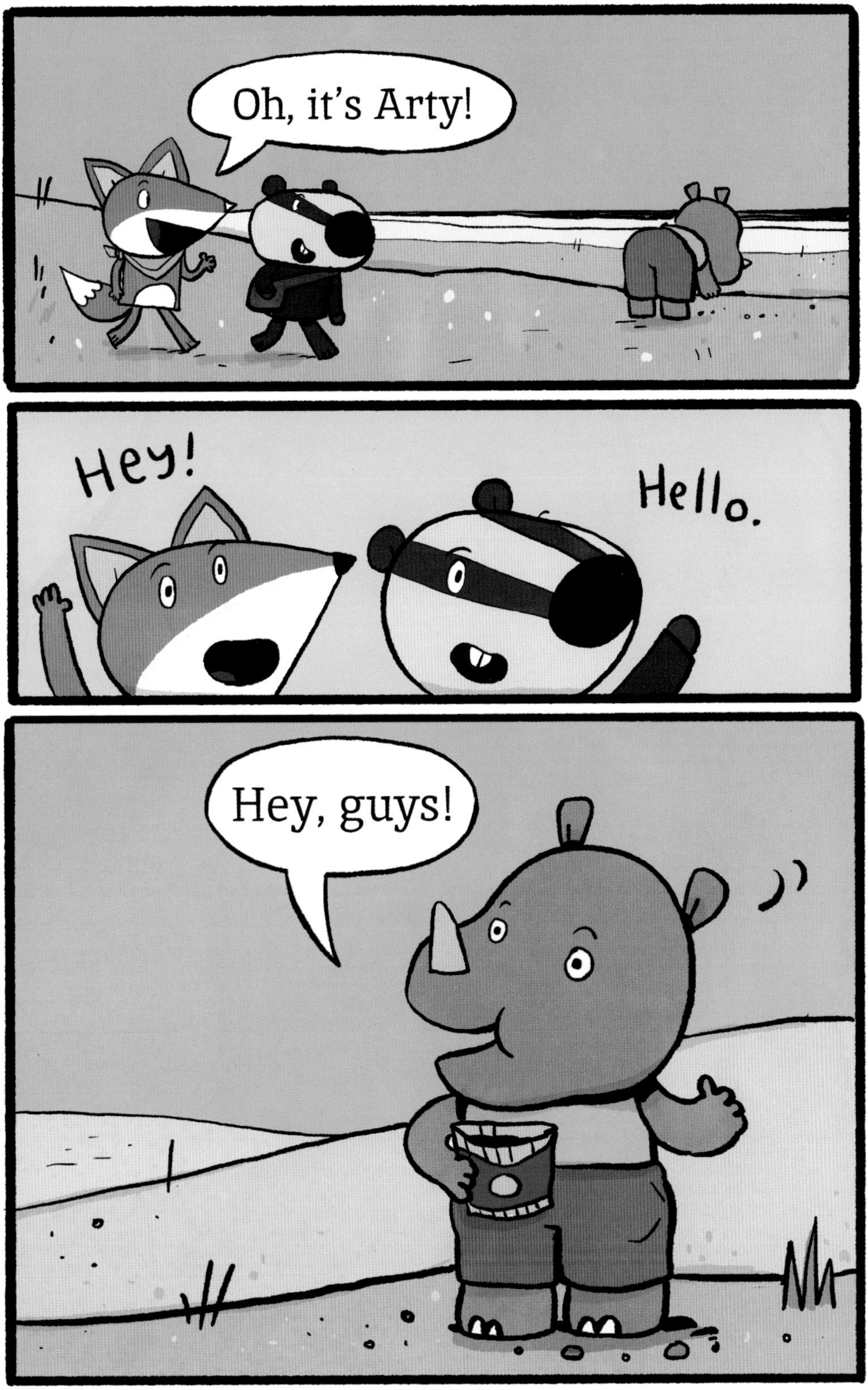
Oh, it's Arty!
Hey!
Hello.
Hey, guys!

Arty

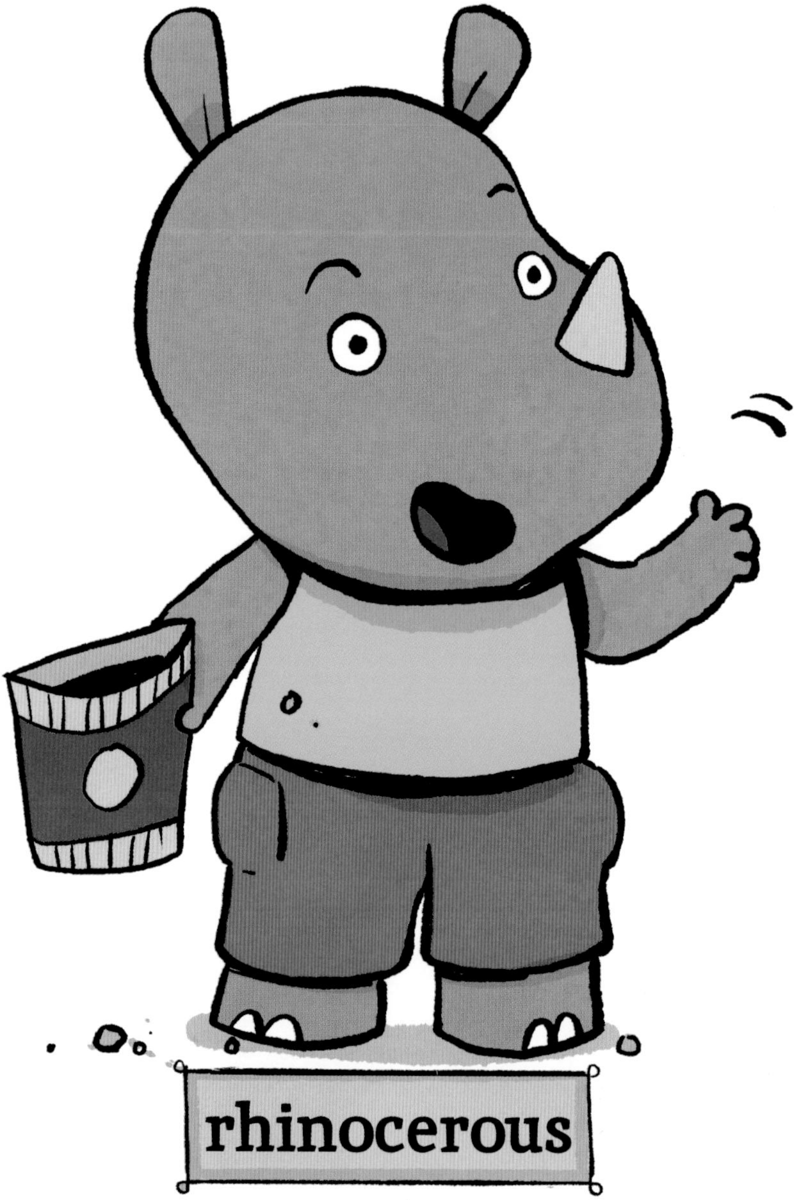

rhinocerous

seaside collector
favorite color: green

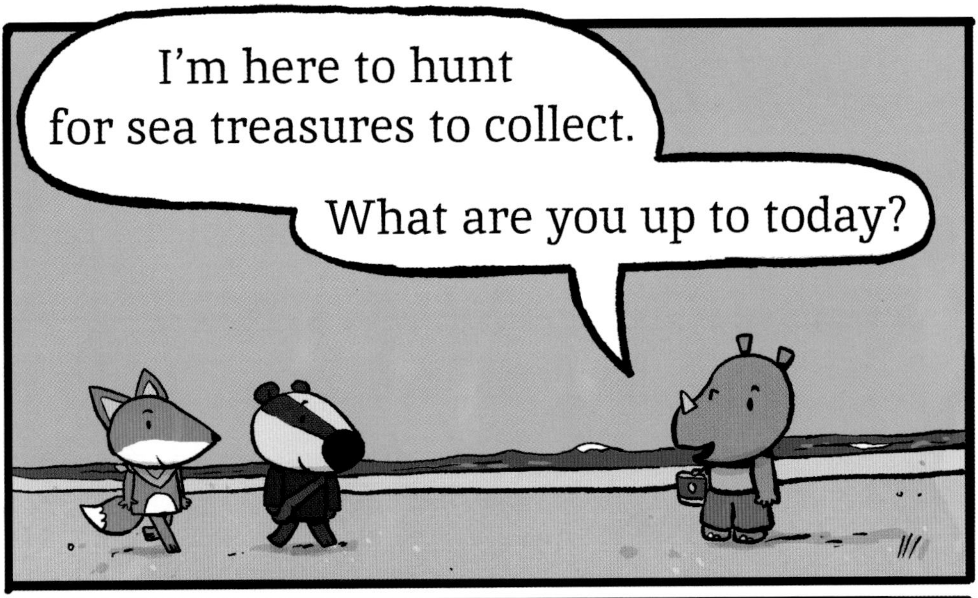
I'm here to hunt for sea treasures to collect.
What are you up to today?

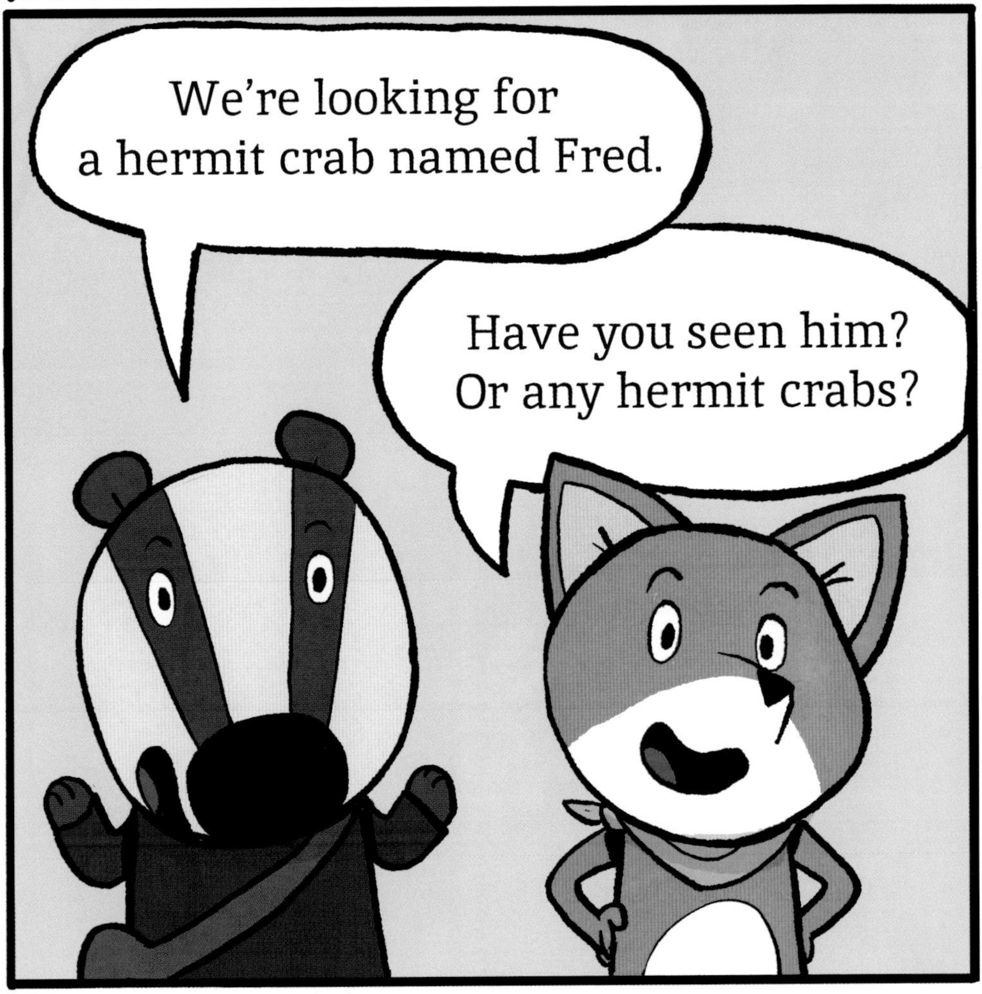
We're looking for a hermit crab named Fred.
Have you seen him? Or any hermit crabs?

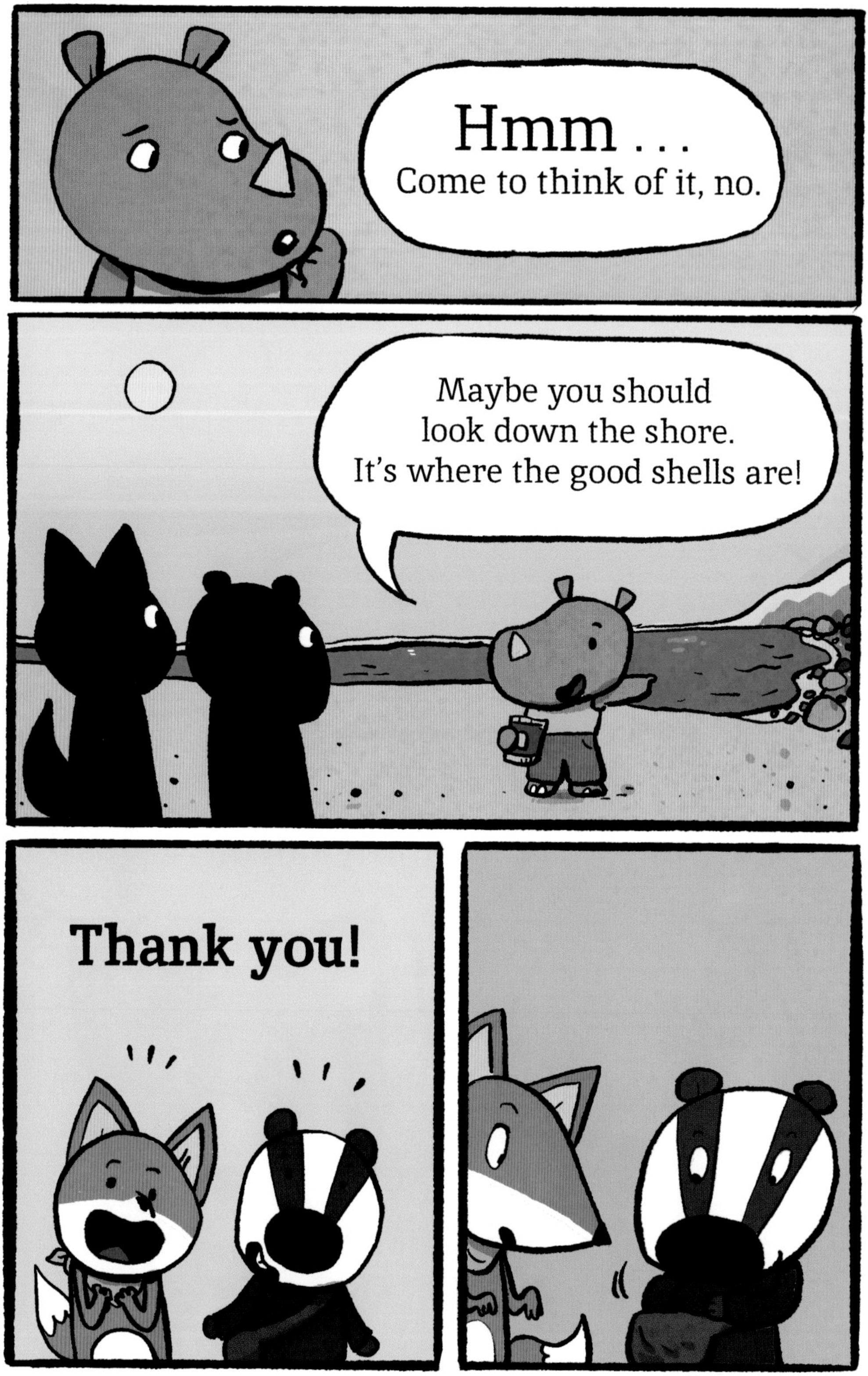
Hmm . . .
Come to think of it, no.
Maybe you should look down the shore. It's where the good shells are!
Thank you!

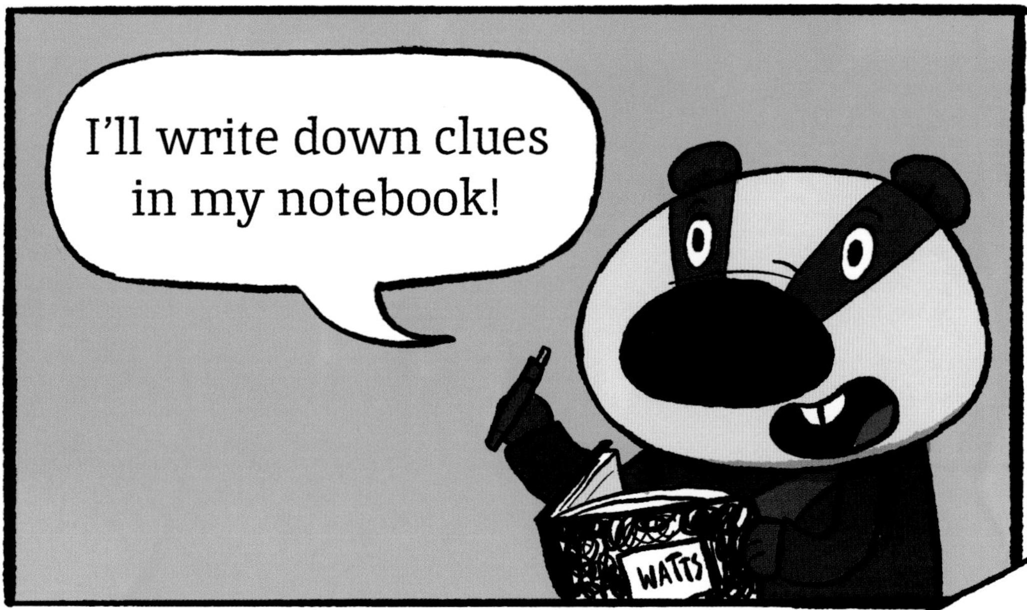
I'll write down clues in my notebook!
WATTS

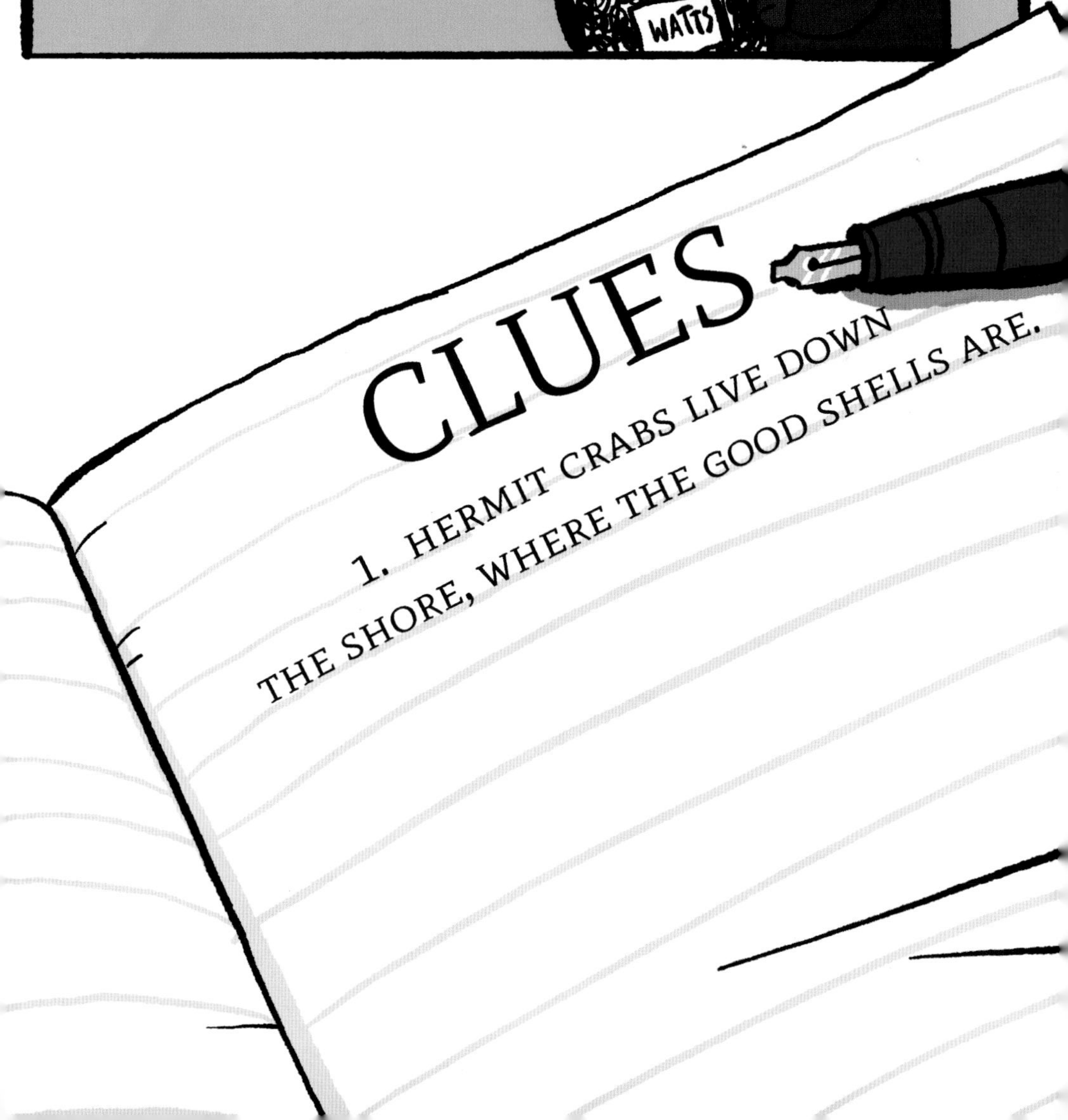
CLUES
1. HERMIT CRABS LIVE DOWN THE SHORE, WHERE THE GOOD SHELLS ARE.

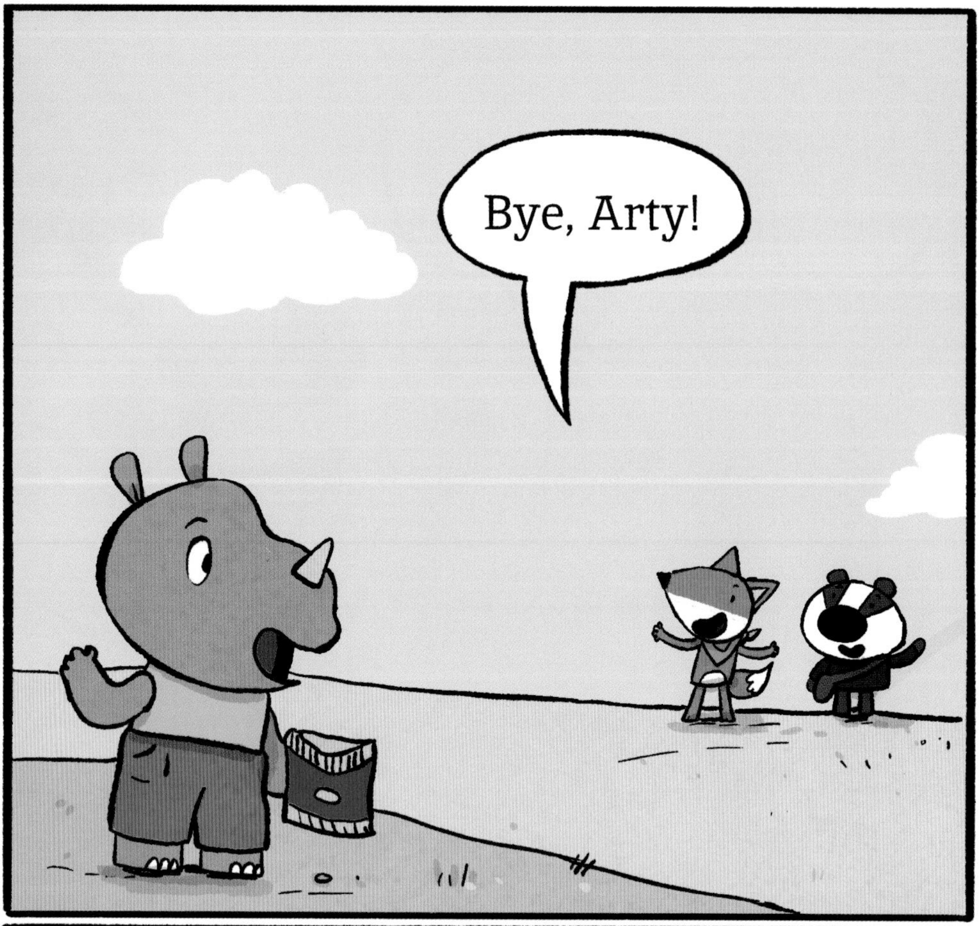
Bye, Arty!

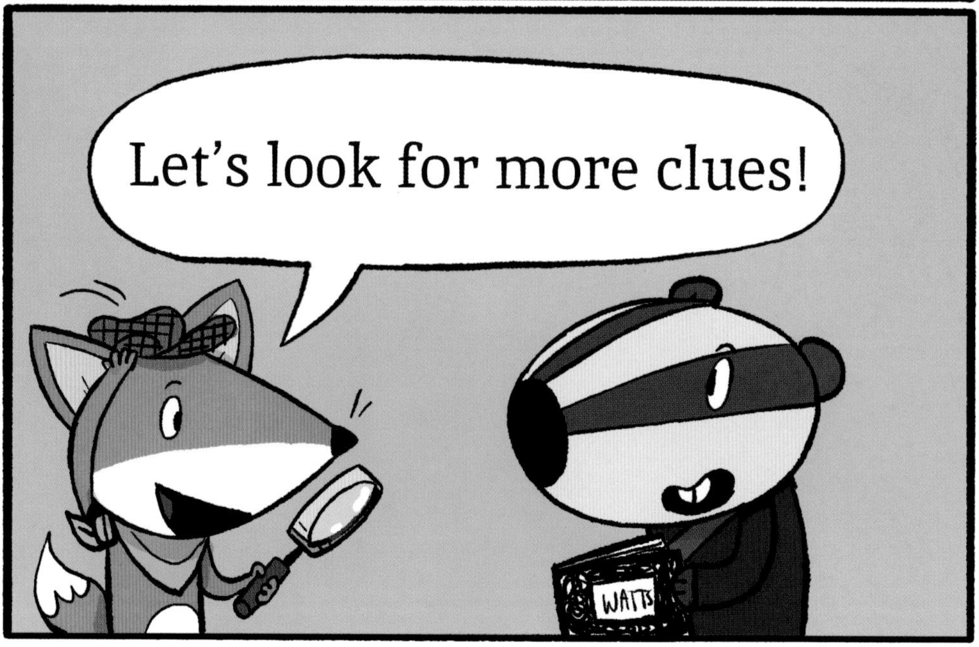
Let's look for more clues!
WATTS

CHAPTER 3

Farther down the shore . . .

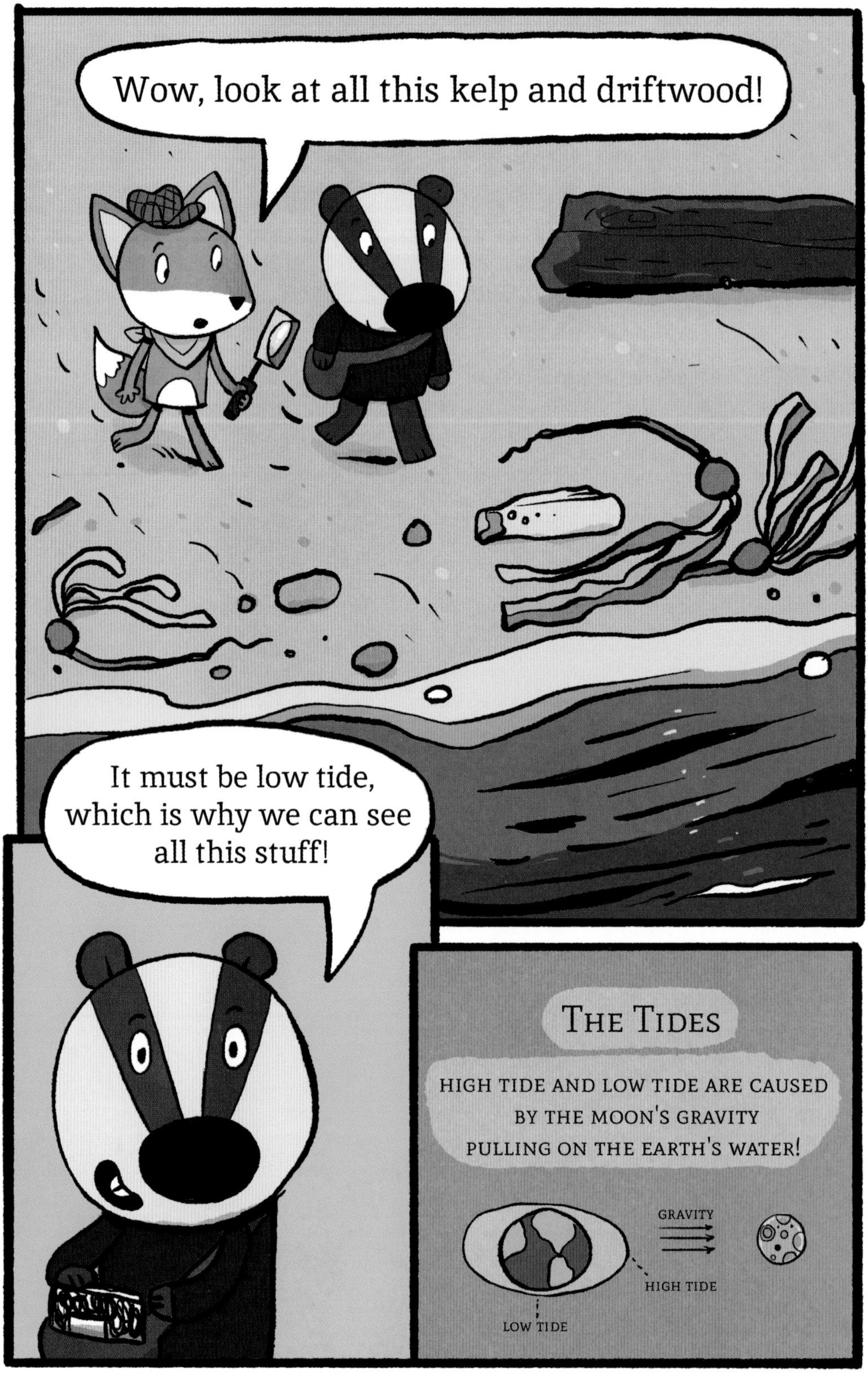
Wow, look at all this kelp and driftwood!
It must be low tide, which is why we can see all this stuff!
THE TIDES
HIGH TIDE AND LOW TIDE ARE CAUSED BY THE MOON'S GRAVITY PULLING ON THE EARTH'S WATER!
GRAVITY
HIGH TIDE
LOW TIDE

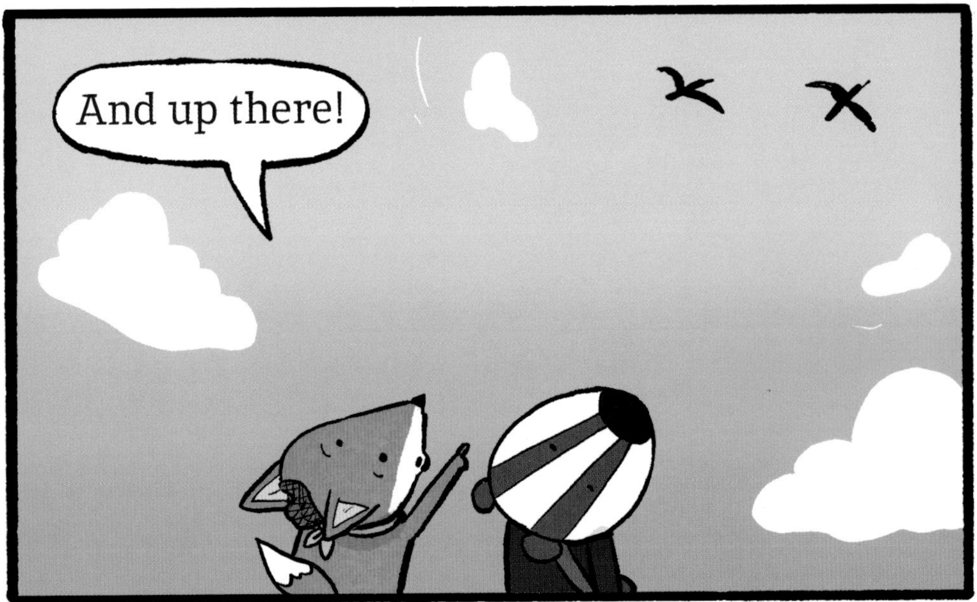
And up there!

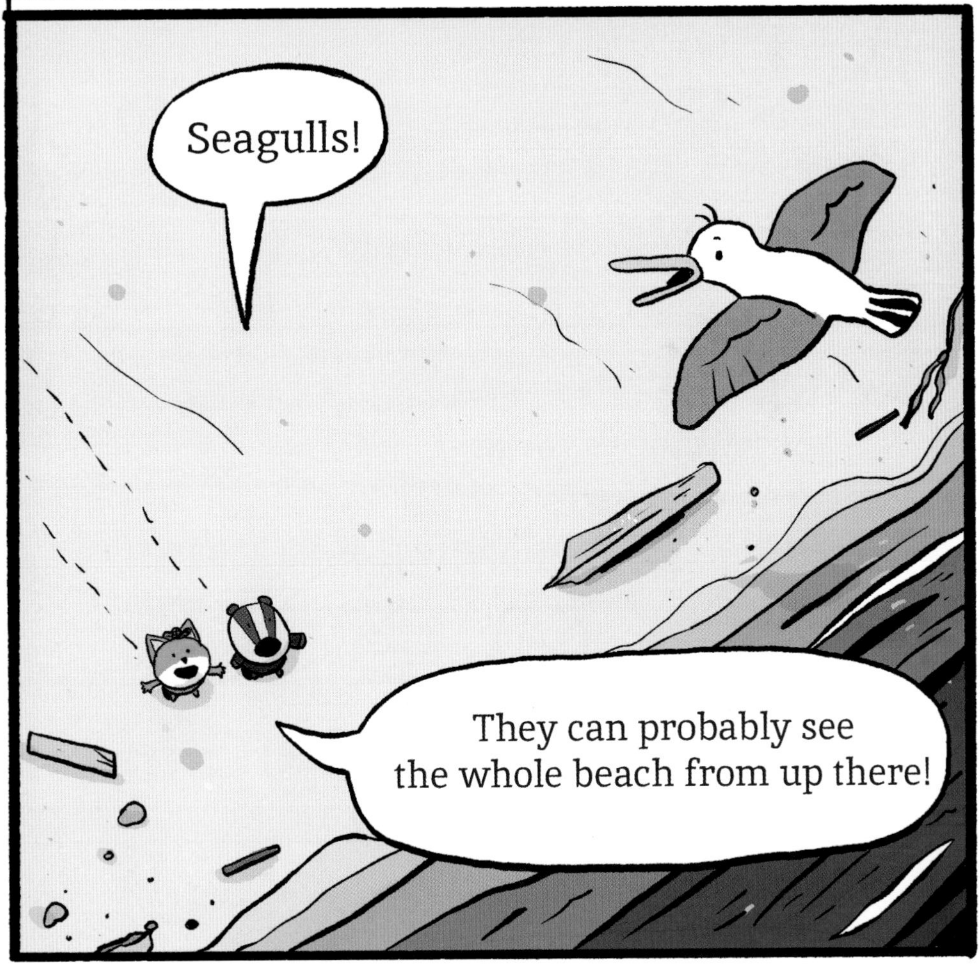
Seagulls!
They can probably see the whole beach from up there!

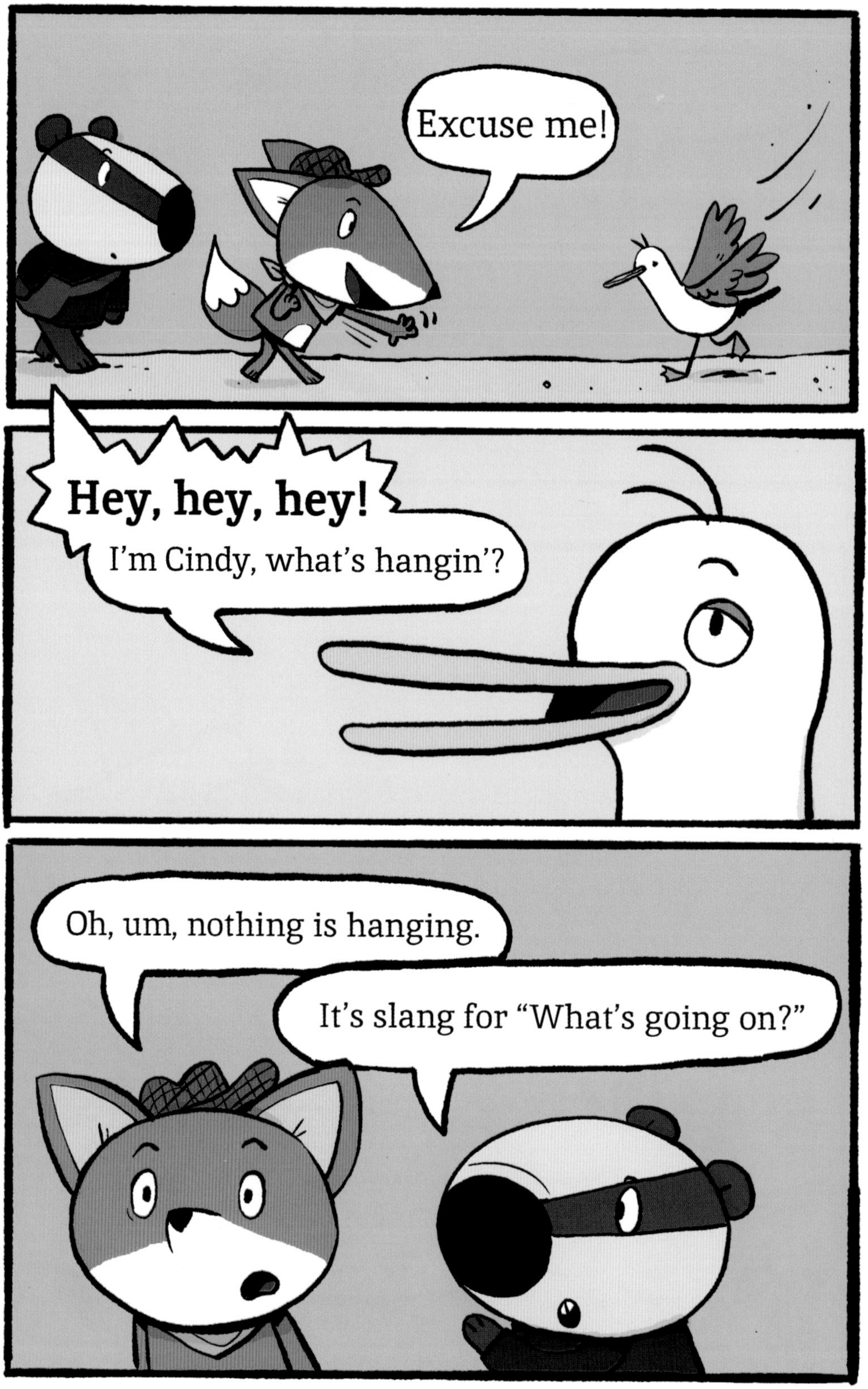
Excuse me!
Hey, hey, hey!
I'm Cindy, what's hangin'?
Oh, um, nothing is hanging.
It's slang for "What's going on?"

Cindy

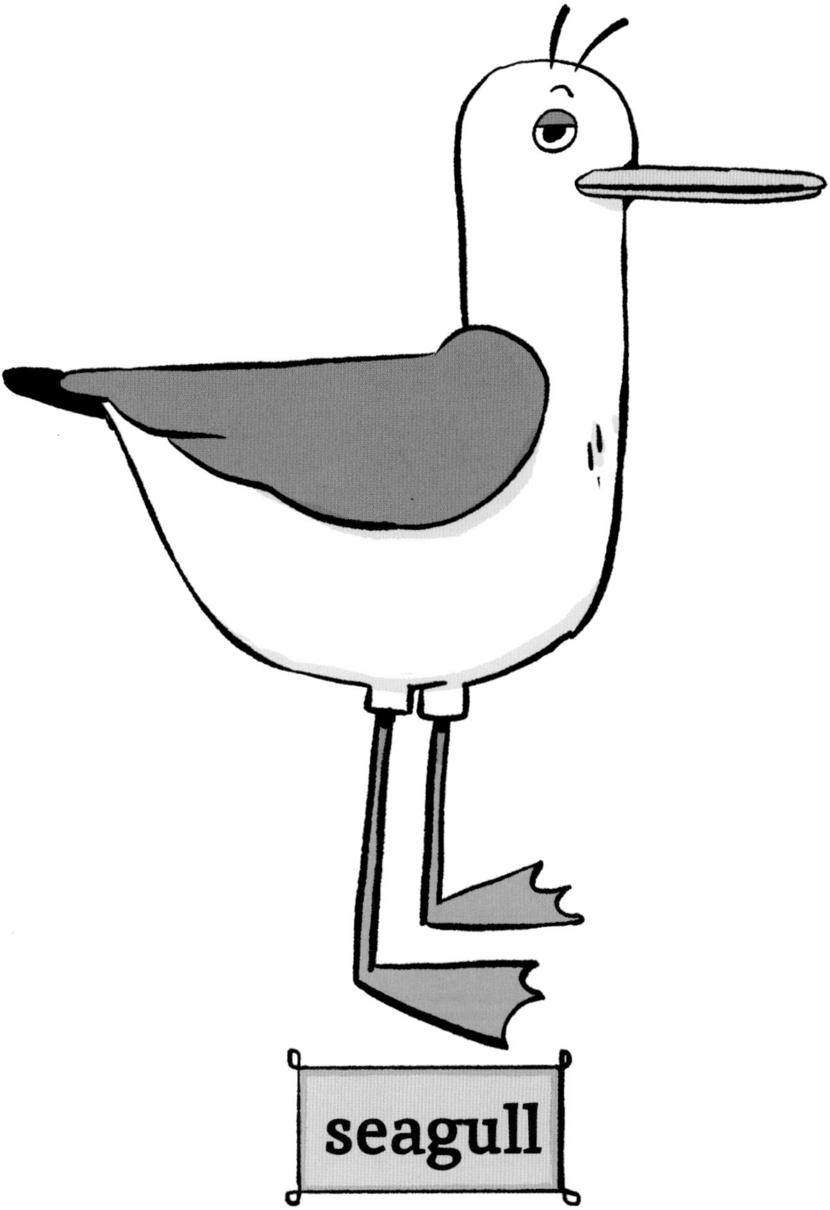
seagull

favorite pastime: surfing waves
favorite color: sky blue

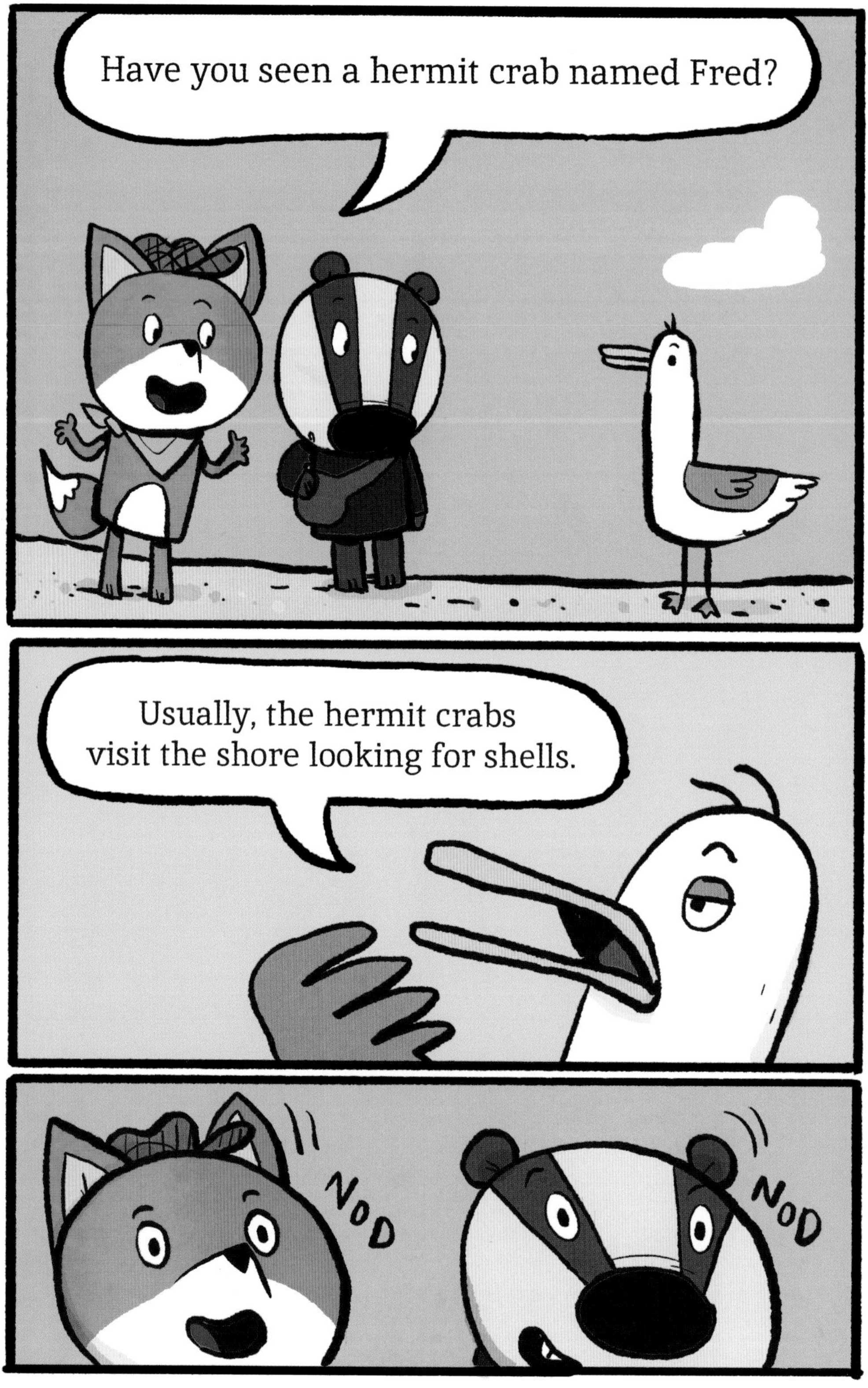

Have you seen a hermit crab named Fred?
Usually, the hermit crabs visit the shore looking for shells.
NOD
NOD

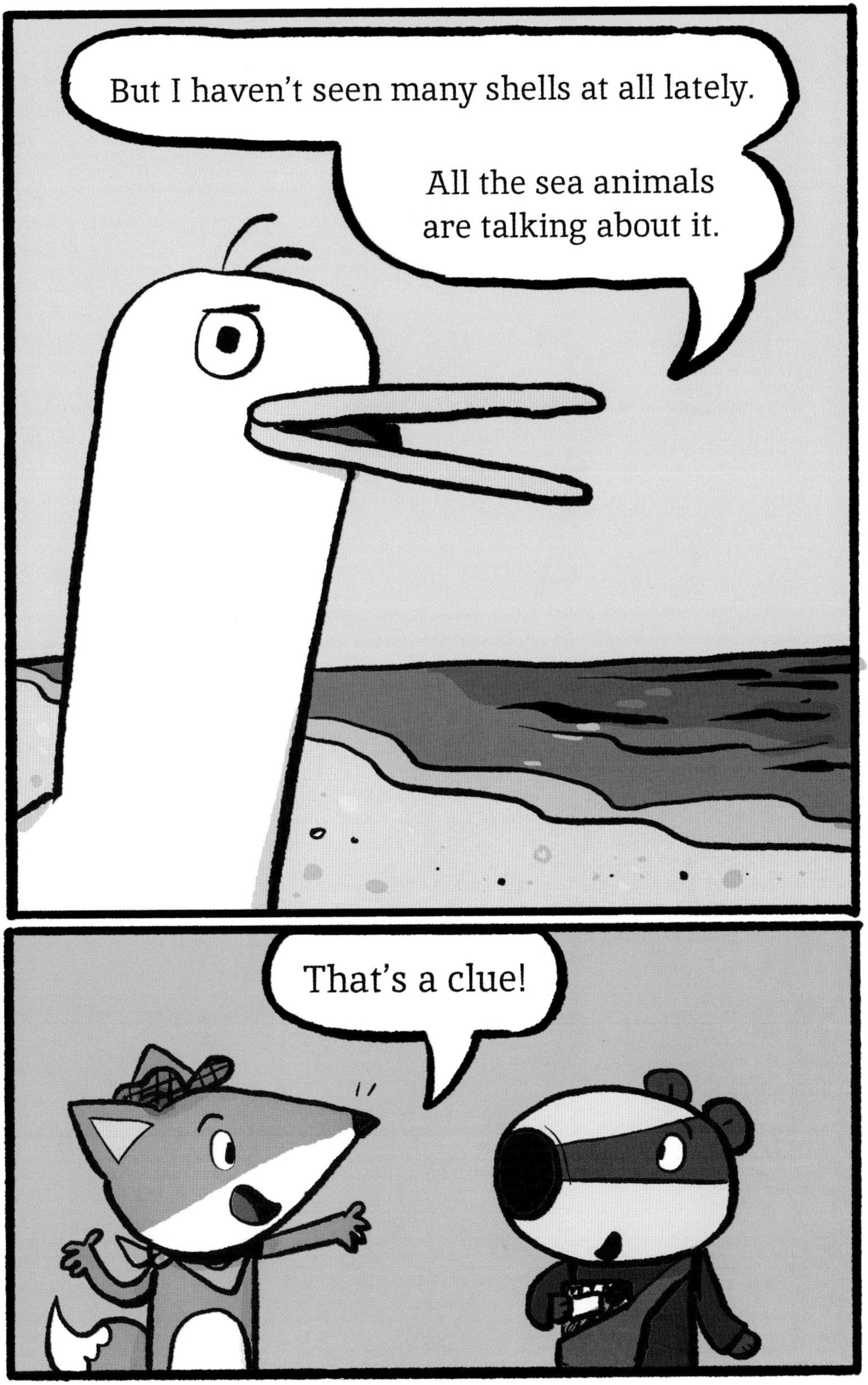
But I haven't seen many shells at all lately.
All the sea animals are talking about it.
That's a clue!

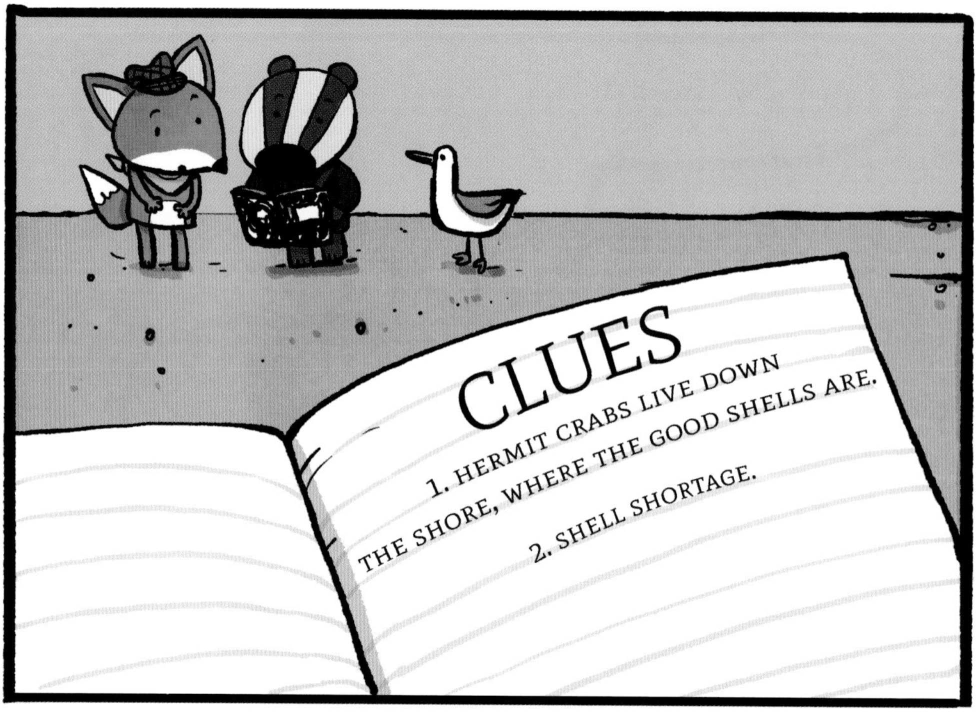
CLUES
1. HERMIT CRABS LIVE DOWN THE SHORE, WHERE THE GOOD SHELLS ARE.
2. SHELL SHORTAGE.

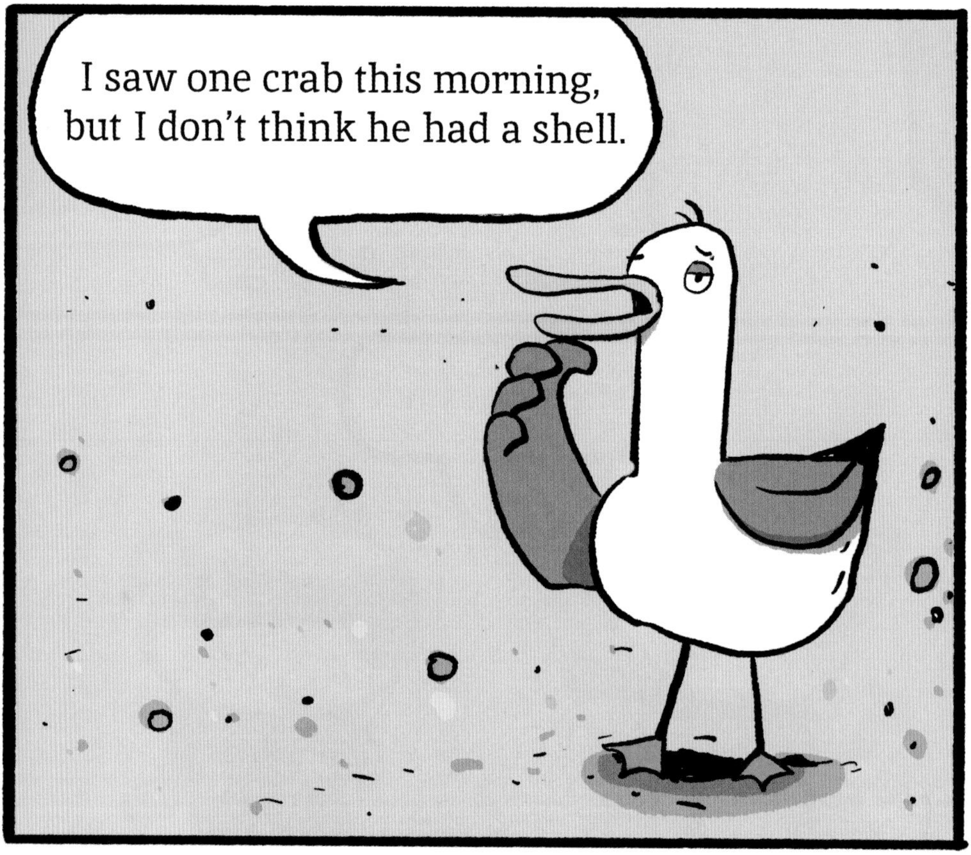
I saw one crab this morning, but I don't think he had a shell.

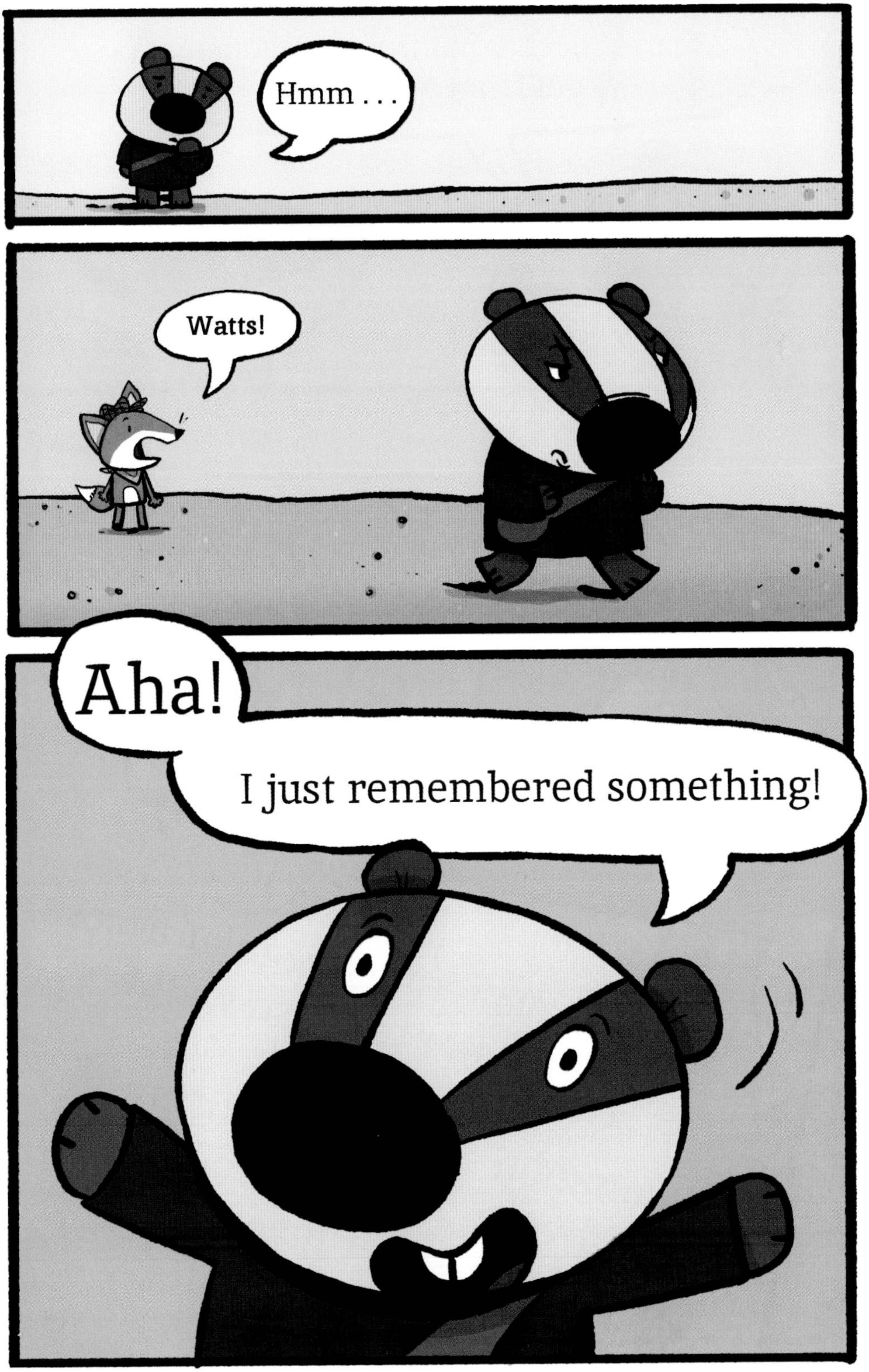
Hmm . . .
Watts!
Aha!
I just remembered something!

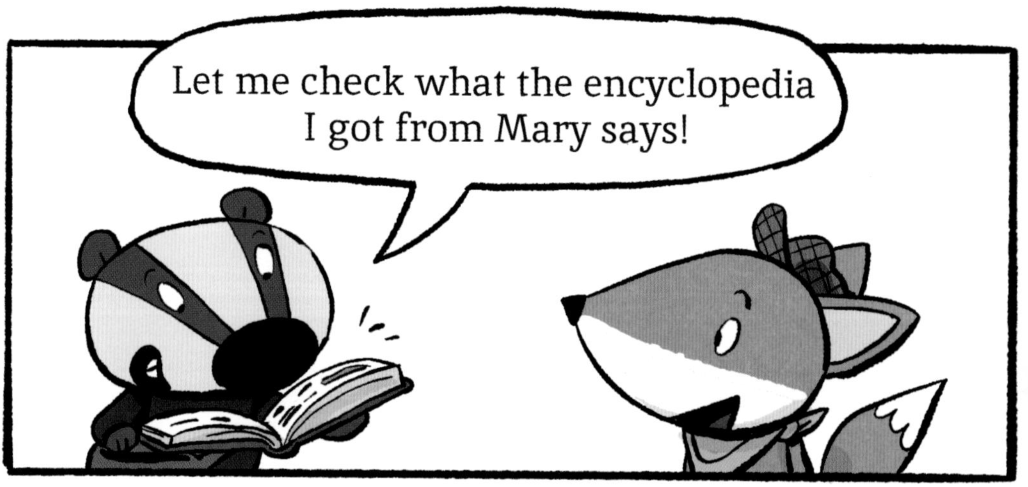
Let me check what the encyclopedia I got from Mary says!

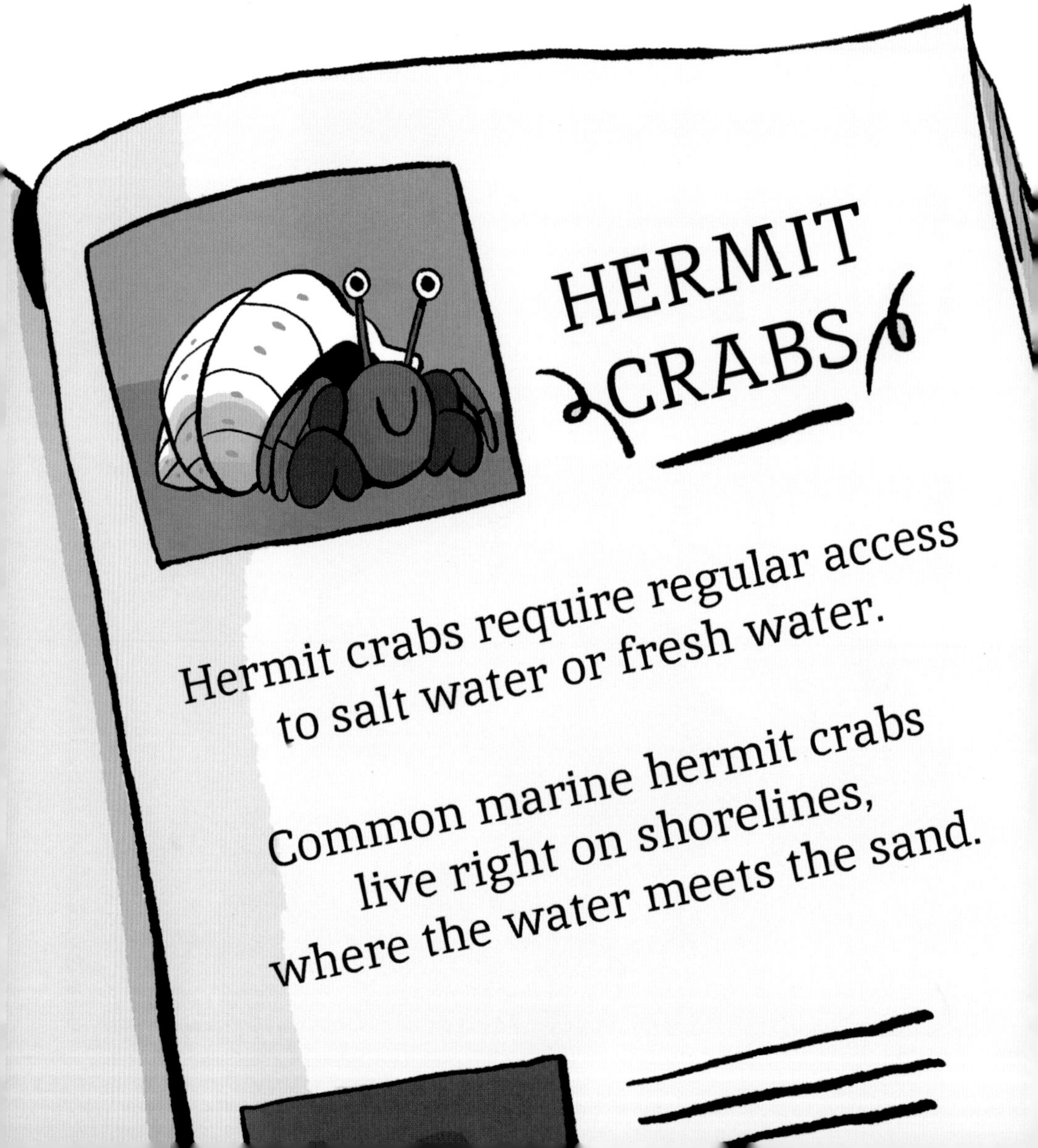
HERMIT CRABS
Hermit crabs require regular access to salt water or fresh water.
Common marine hermit crabs live right on shorelines, where the water meets the sand.

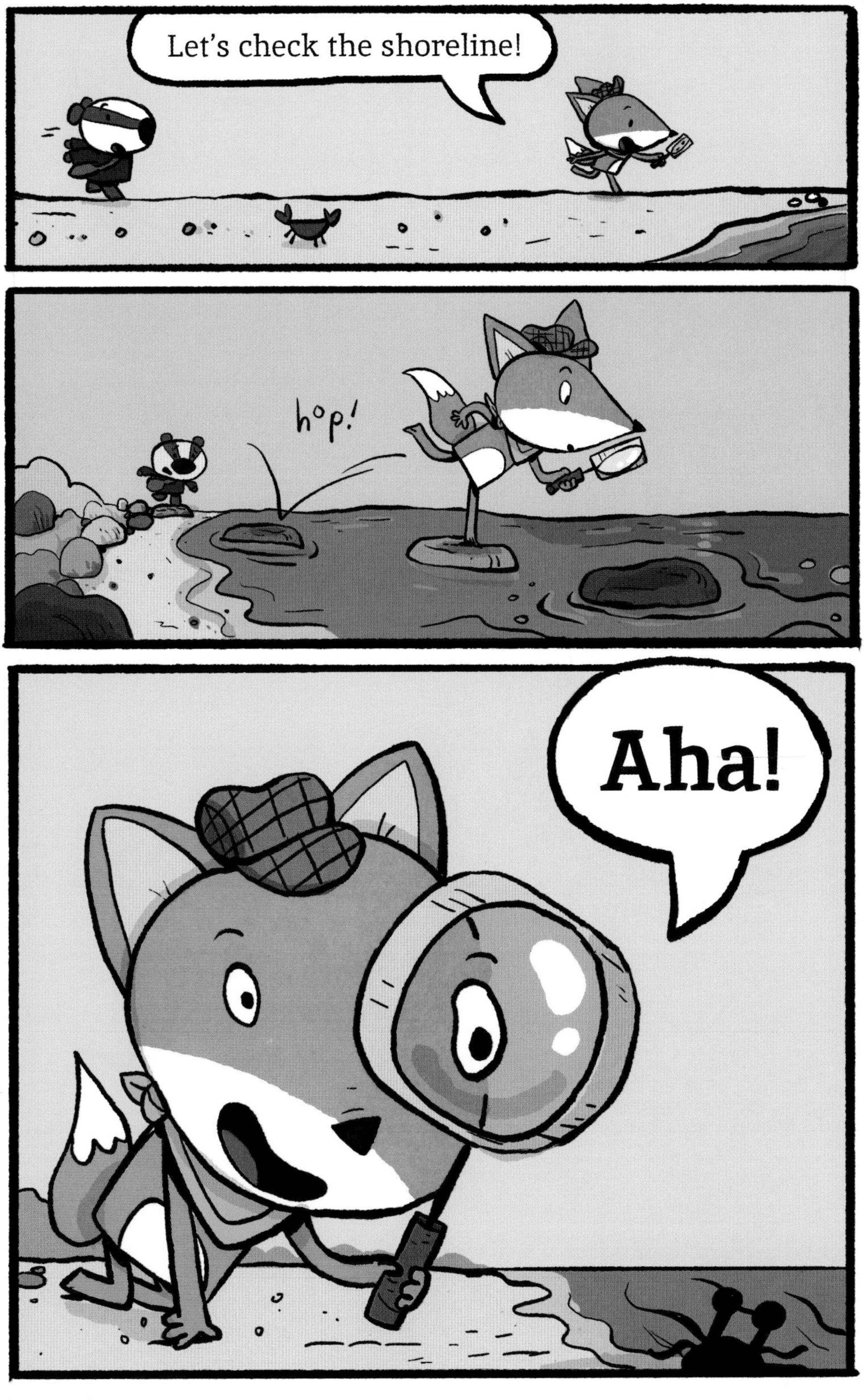
Let's check the shoreline!
hop!
Aha!

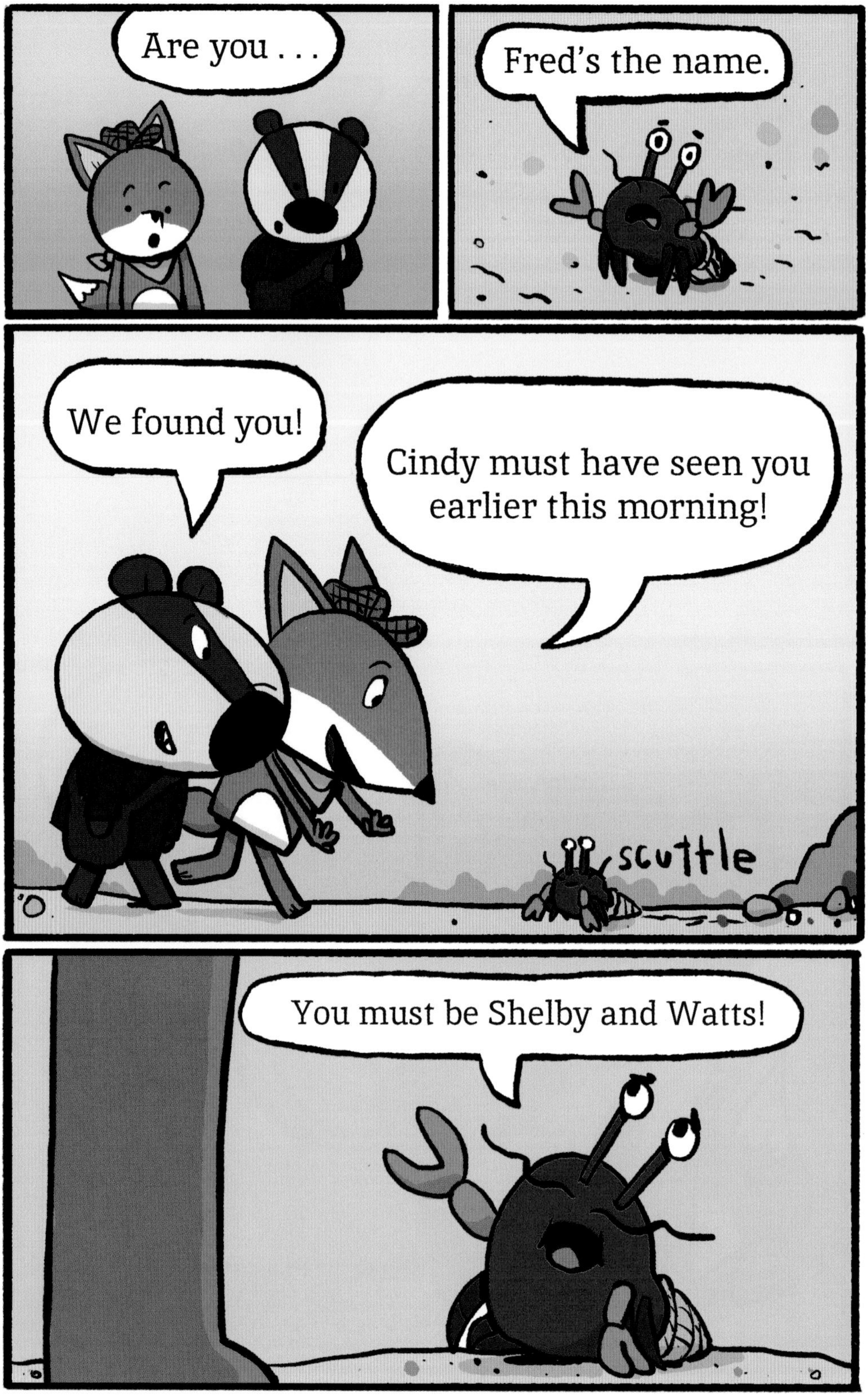
Are you . . .
Fred's the name.
We found you!
Cindy must have seen you earlier this morning!
scuttle
You must be Shelby and Watts!

Fred

hermit crab

current mood: very squished
favorite color: red

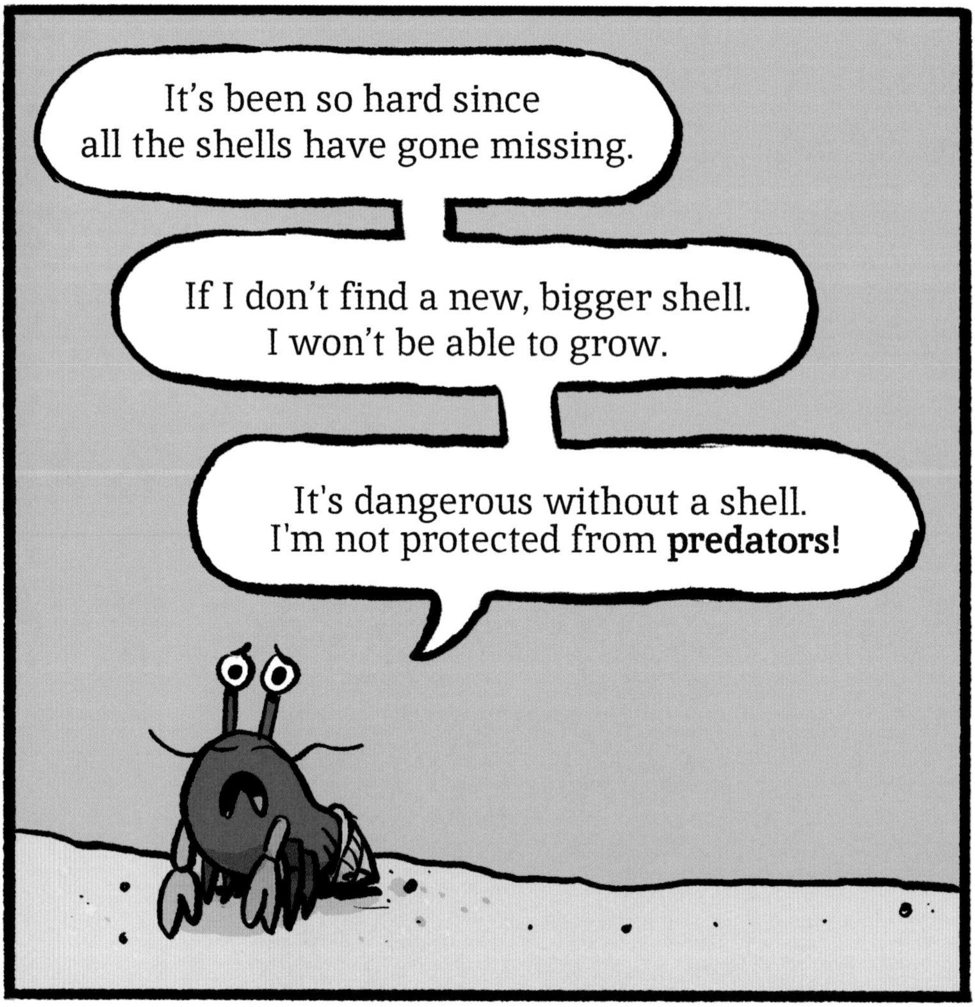
It's been so hard since all the shells have gone missing.
If I don't find a new, bigger shell. I won't be able to grow.
It's dangerous without a shell. I'm not protected from **predators!**

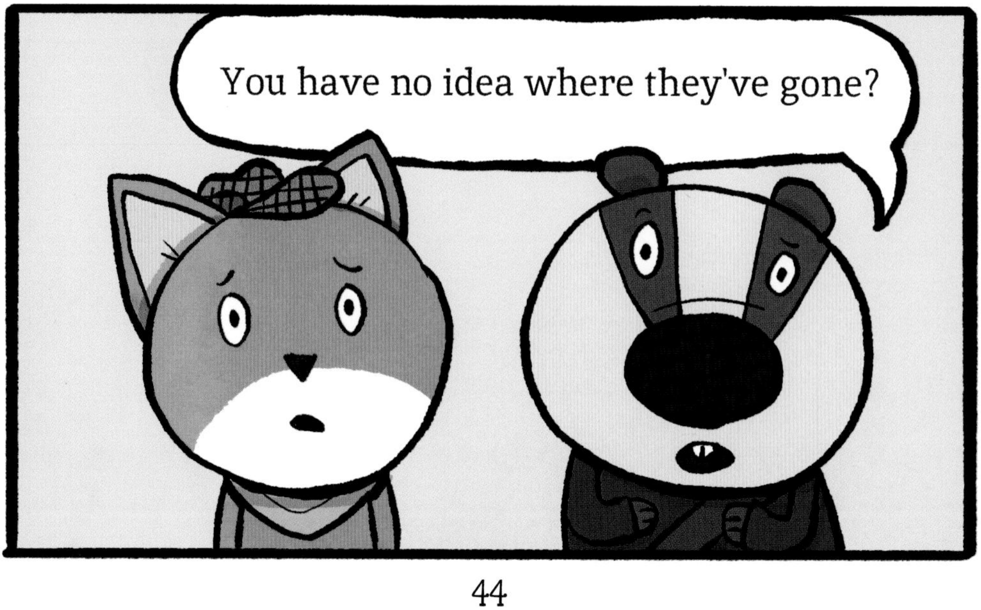
You have no idea where they've gone?

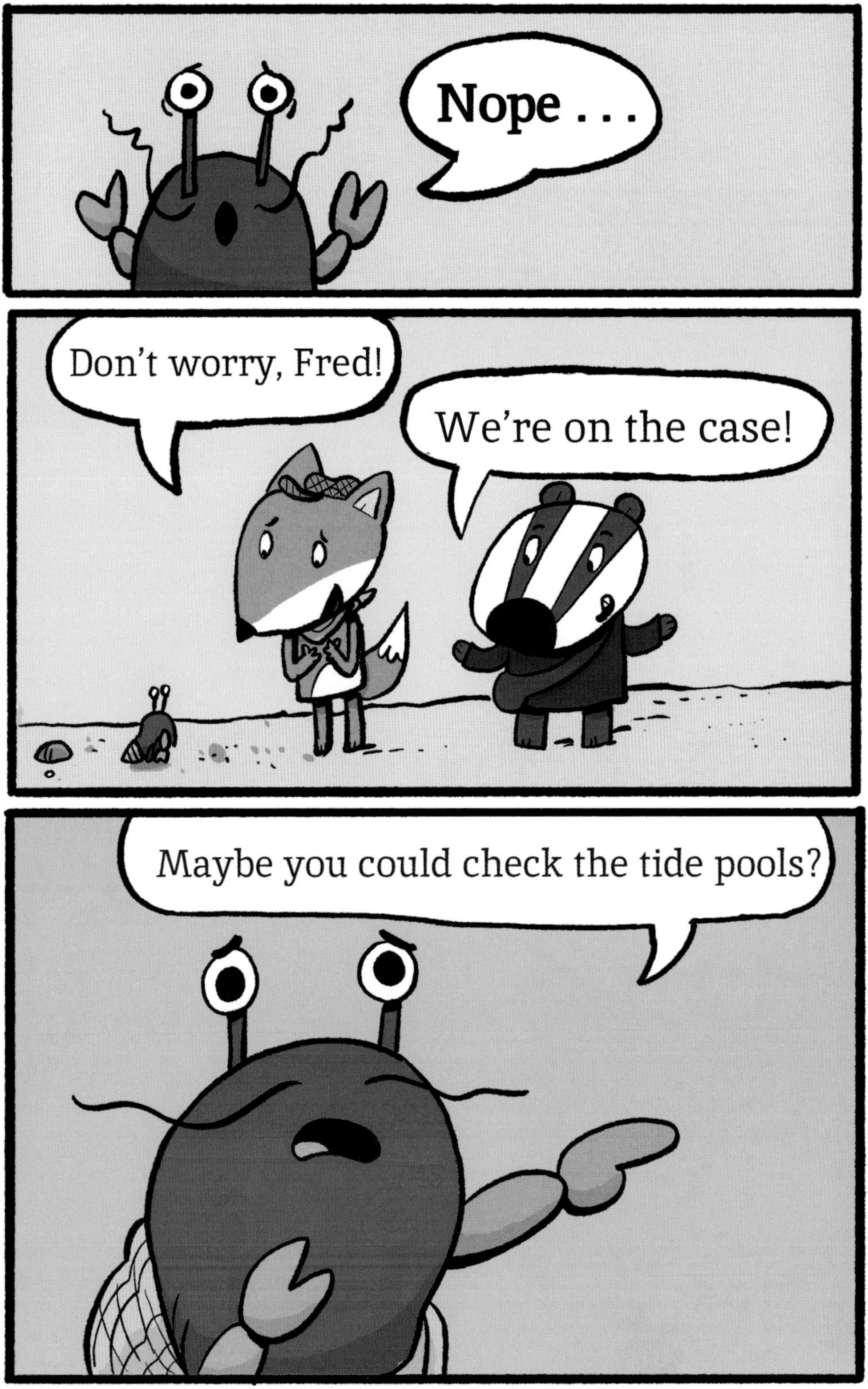
Nope . . .
Don't worry, Fred!
We're on the case!
Maybe you could check the tide pools?

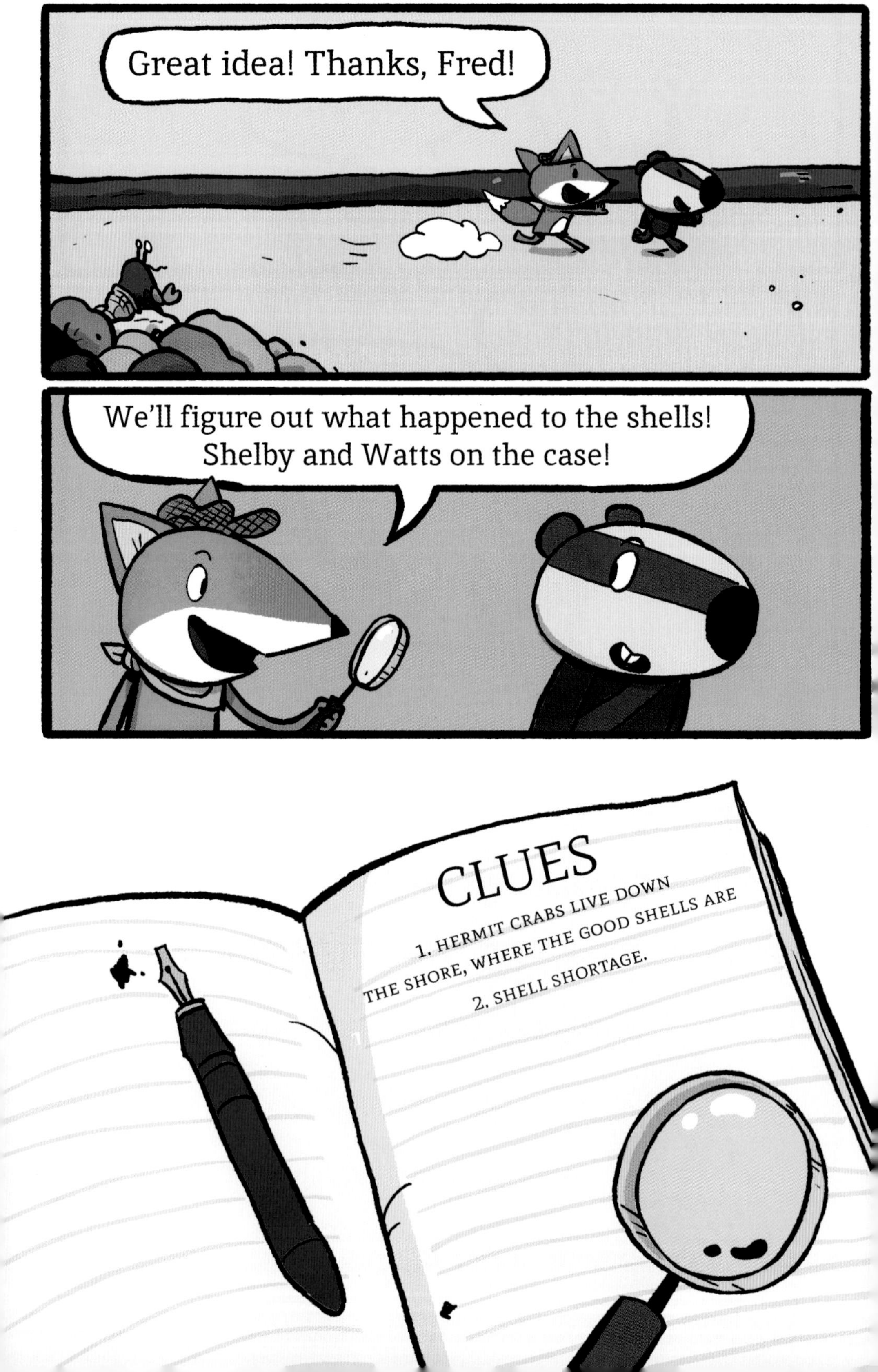
Great idea! Thanks, Fred!
We'll figure out what happened to the shells! Shelby and Watts on the case!
CLUES
1. HERMIT CRABS LIVE DOWN THE SHORE, WHERE THE GOOD SHELLS ARE
2. SHELL SHORTAGE.

CHAPTER 4

At the rocky tide pools . . .

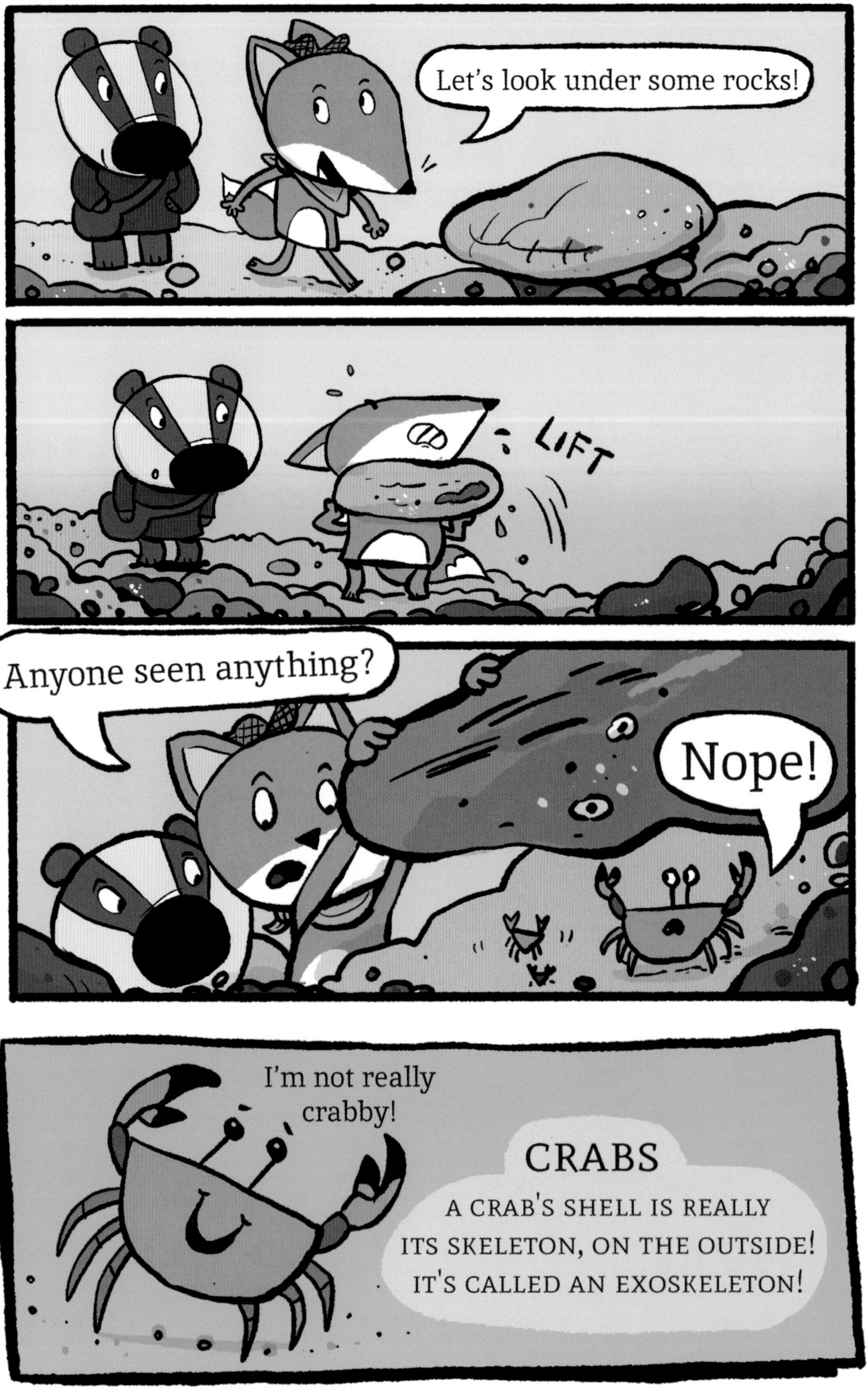
Let's look under some rocks!
LIFT
Anyone seen anything?
Nope!
I'm not really crabby!
CRABS
A CRAB'S SHELL IS REALLY ITS SKELETON, ON THE OUTSIDE! IT'S CALLED AN EXOSKELETON!

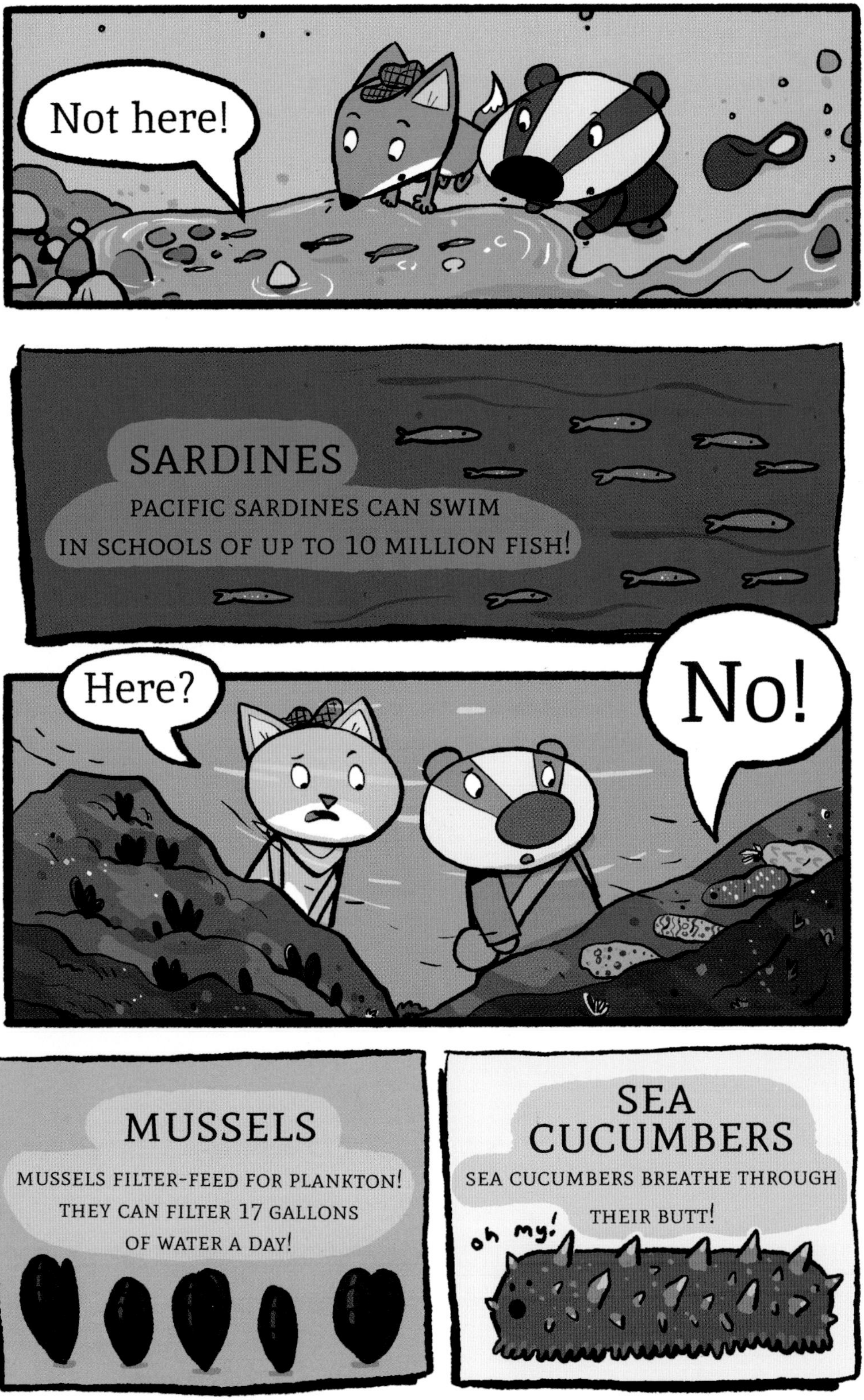
Not here!
SARDINES
PACIFIC SARDINES CAN SWIM
IN SCHOOLS OF UP TO 10 MILLION FISH!
Here?
No!
MUSSELS
MUSSELS FILTER-FEED FOR PLANKTON!
THEY CAN FILTER 17 GALLONS
OF WATER A DAY!
SEA CUCUMBERS
SEA CUCUMBERS BREATHE THROUGH
THEIR BUTT!
oh my!

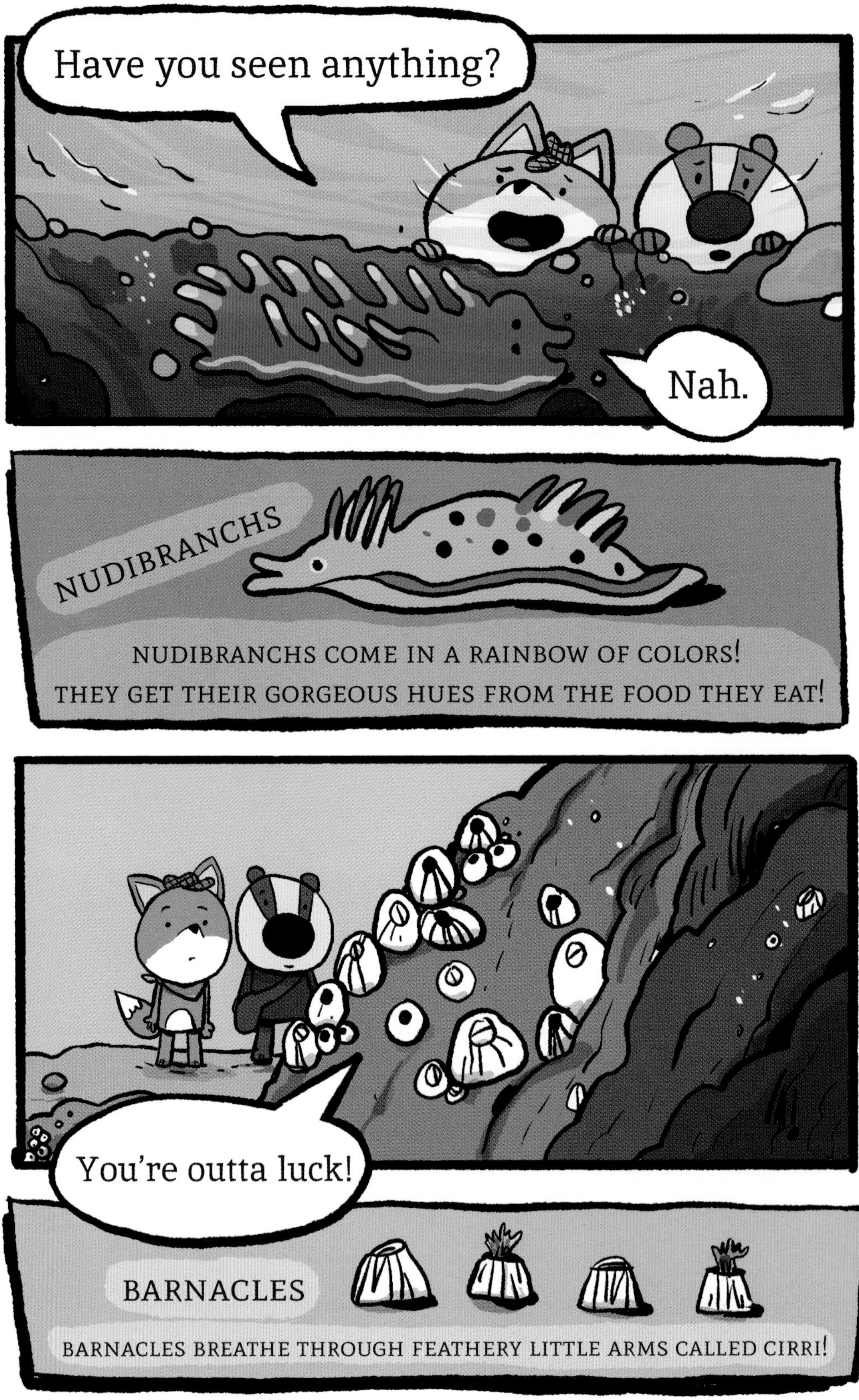
Have you seen anything?
Nah.
NUDIBRANCHS
NUDIBRANCHS COME IN A RAINBOW OF COLORS!
THEY GET THEIR GORGEOUS HUES FROM THE FOOD THEY EAT!
You're outta luck!
BARNACLES
BARNACLES BREATHE THROUGH FEATHERY LITTLE ARMS CALLED CIRRI!

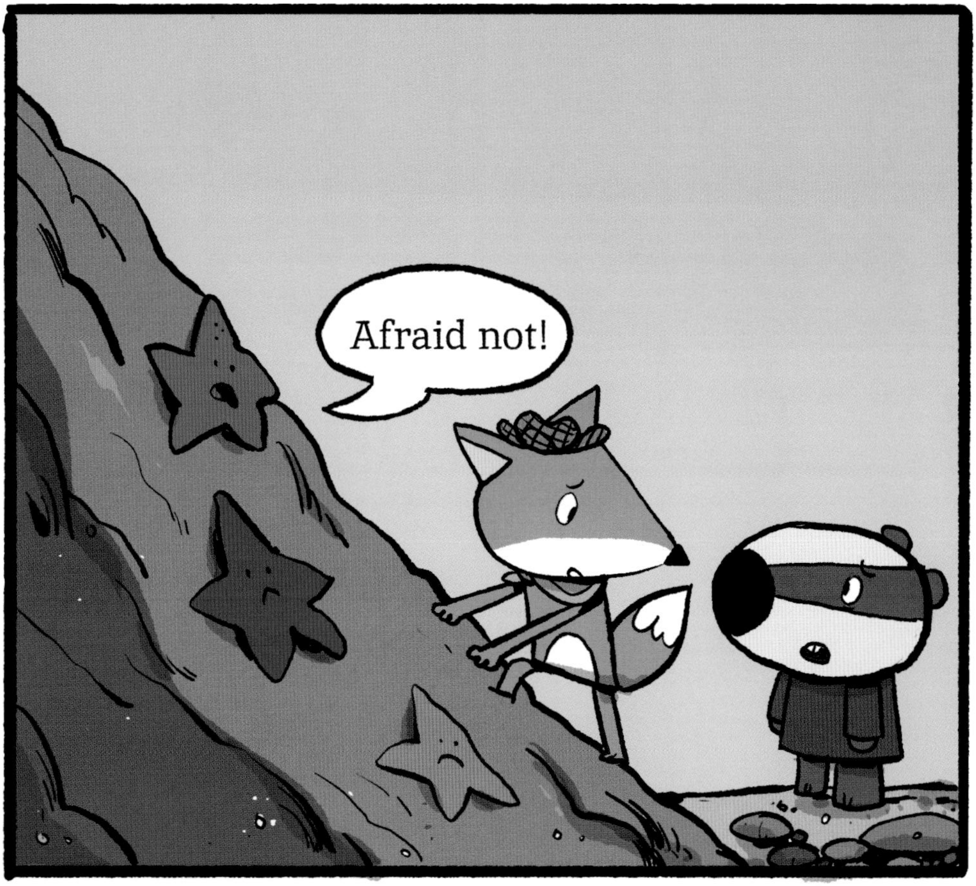
Afraid not!

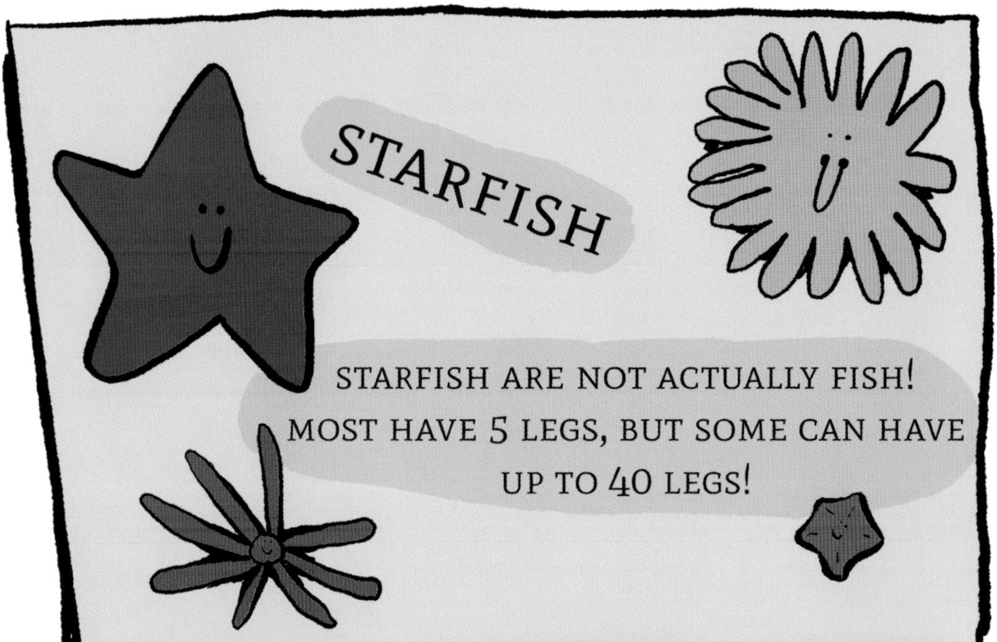
STARFISH
STARFISH ARE NOT ACTUALLY FISH! MOST HAVE 5 LEGS, BUT SOME CAN HAVE UP TO 40 LEGS!

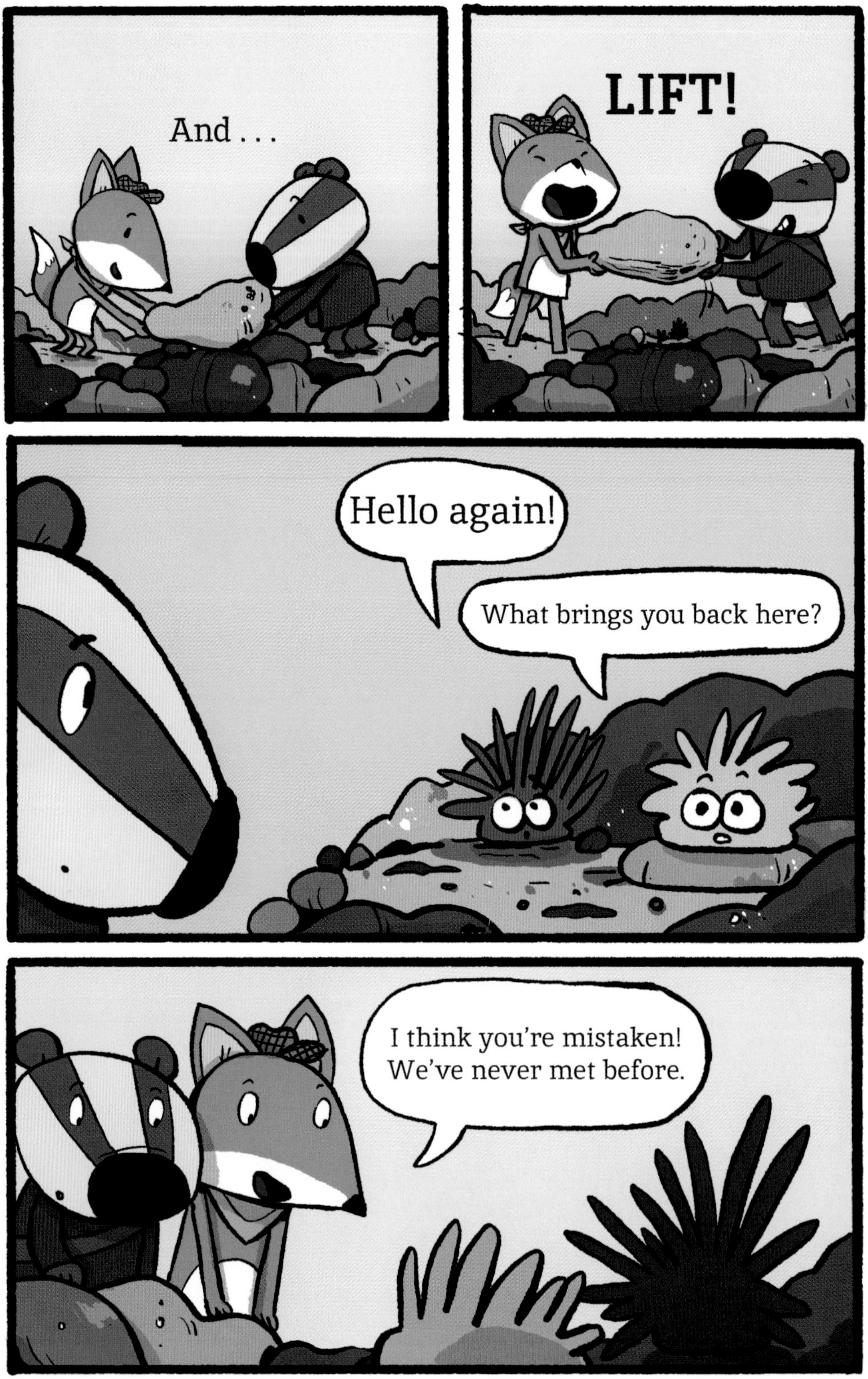
And . . .
LIFT!
Hello again!
What brings you back here?
I think you're mistaken! We've never met before.

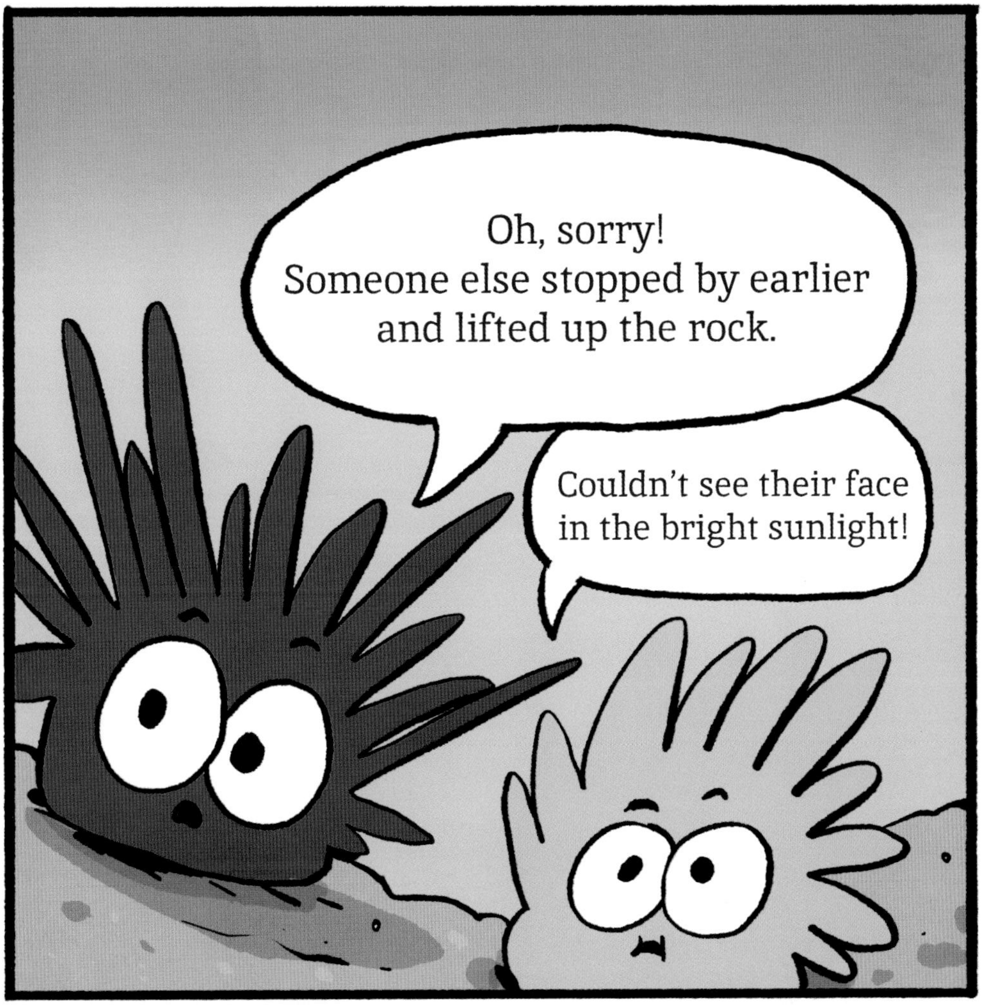
Oh, sorry!
Someone else stopped by earlier
and lifted up the rock.
Couldn't see their face
in the bright sunlight!

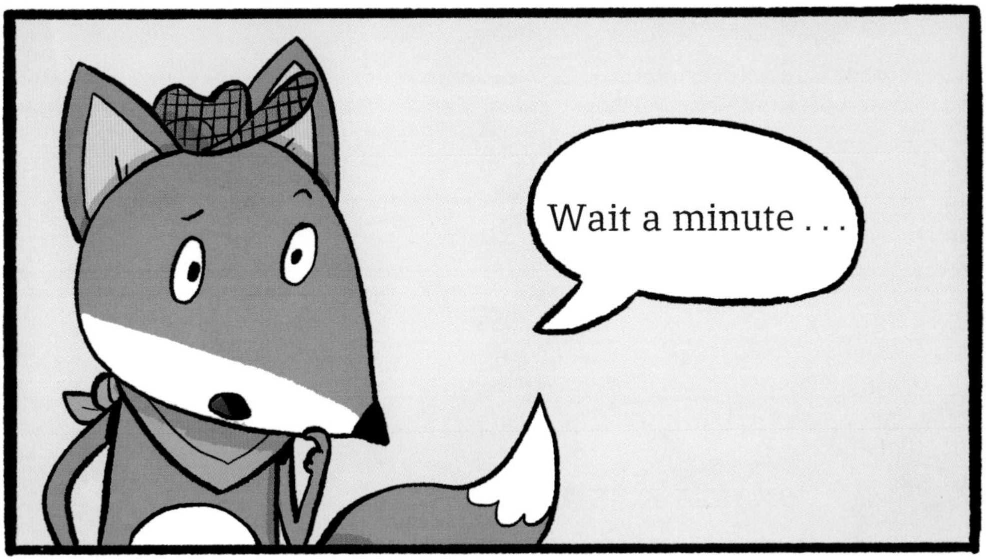
Wait a minute . . .

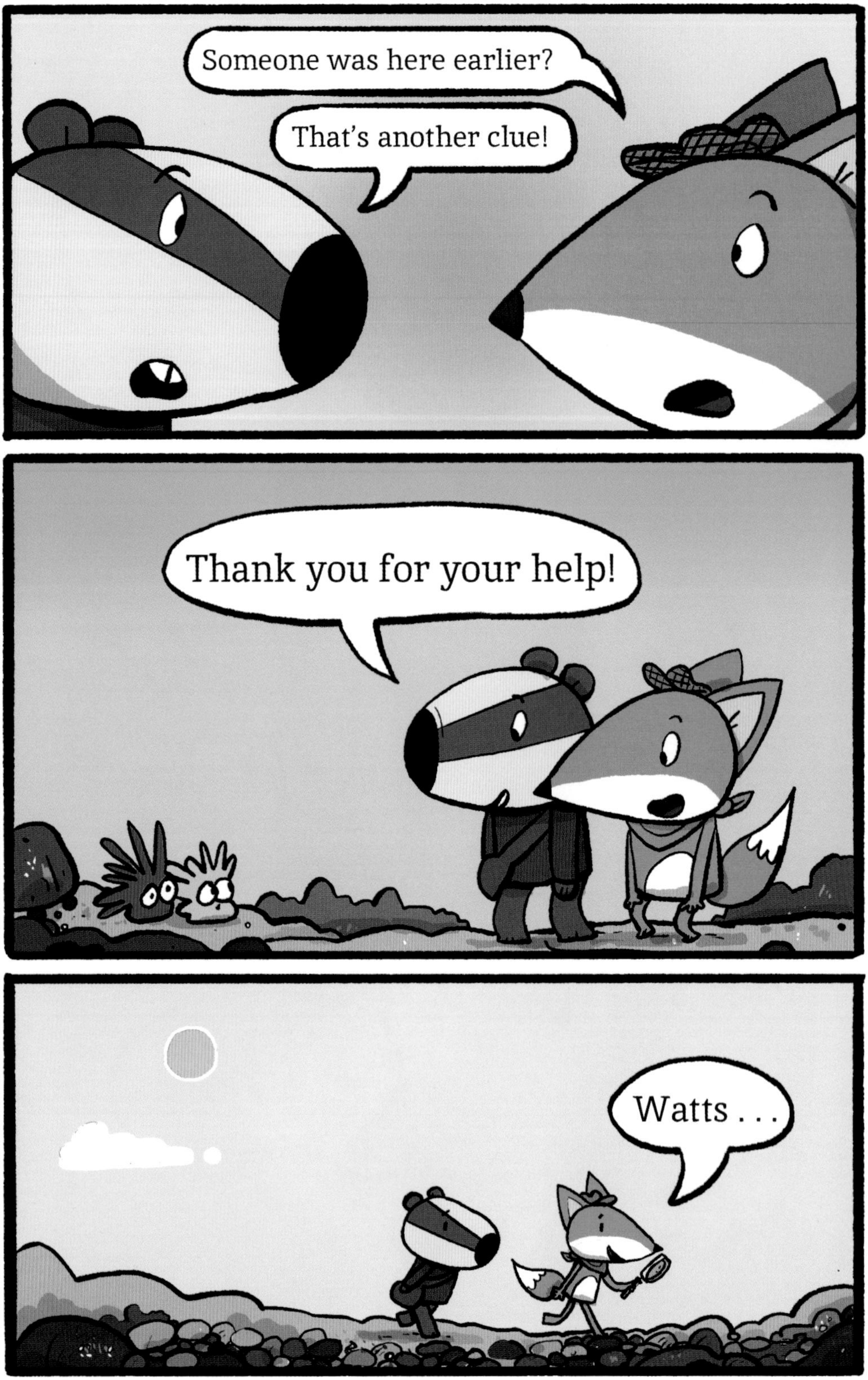
Someone was here earlier?
That's another clue!
Thank you for your help!
Watts . . .

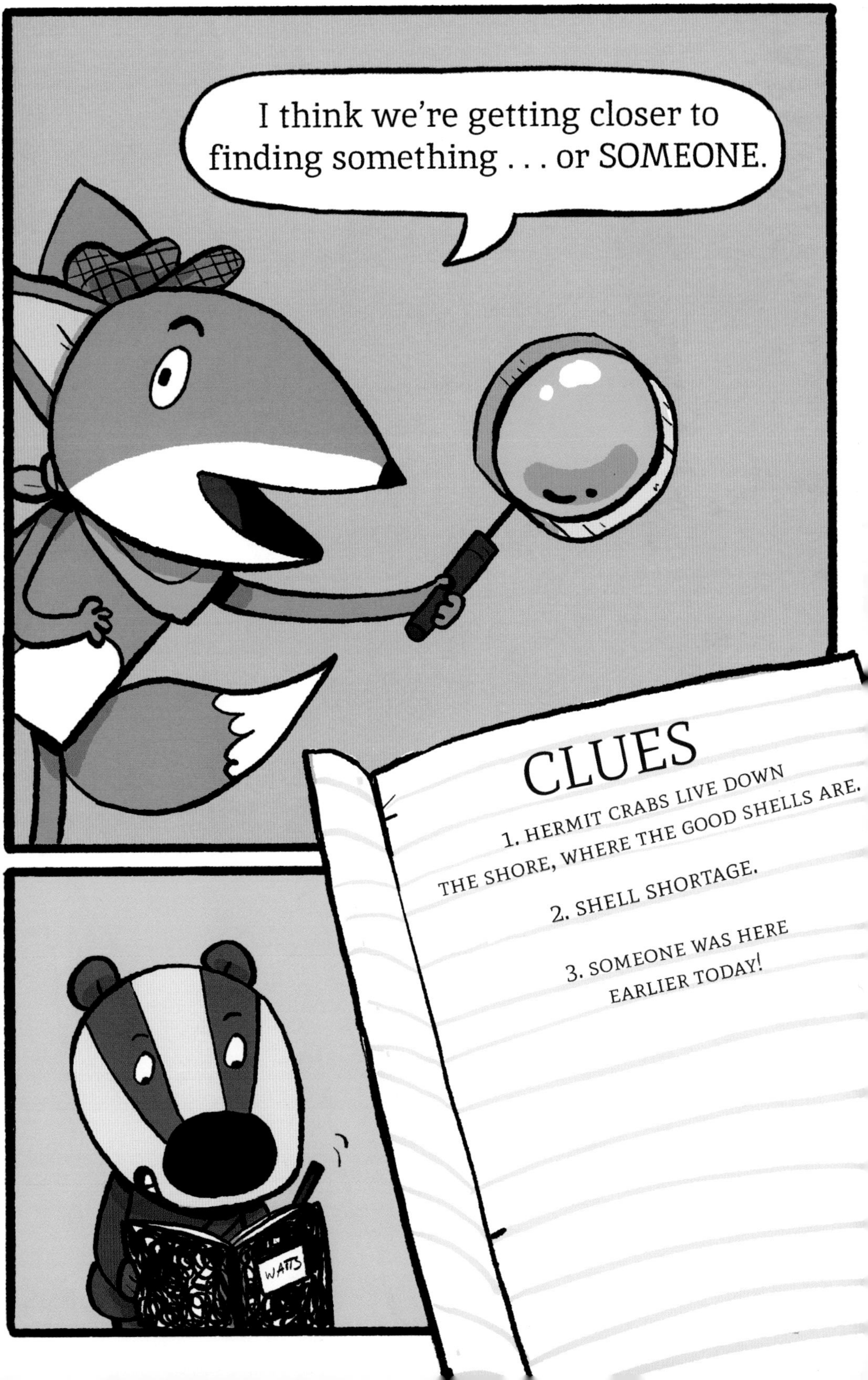

I think we're getting closer to finding something . . . or SOMEONE.
CLUES
1. HERMIT CRABS LIVE DOWN THE SHORE, WHERE THE GOOD SHELLS ARE.
2. SHELL SHORTAGE.
3. SOMEONE WAS HERE EARLIER TODAY!
WATTS

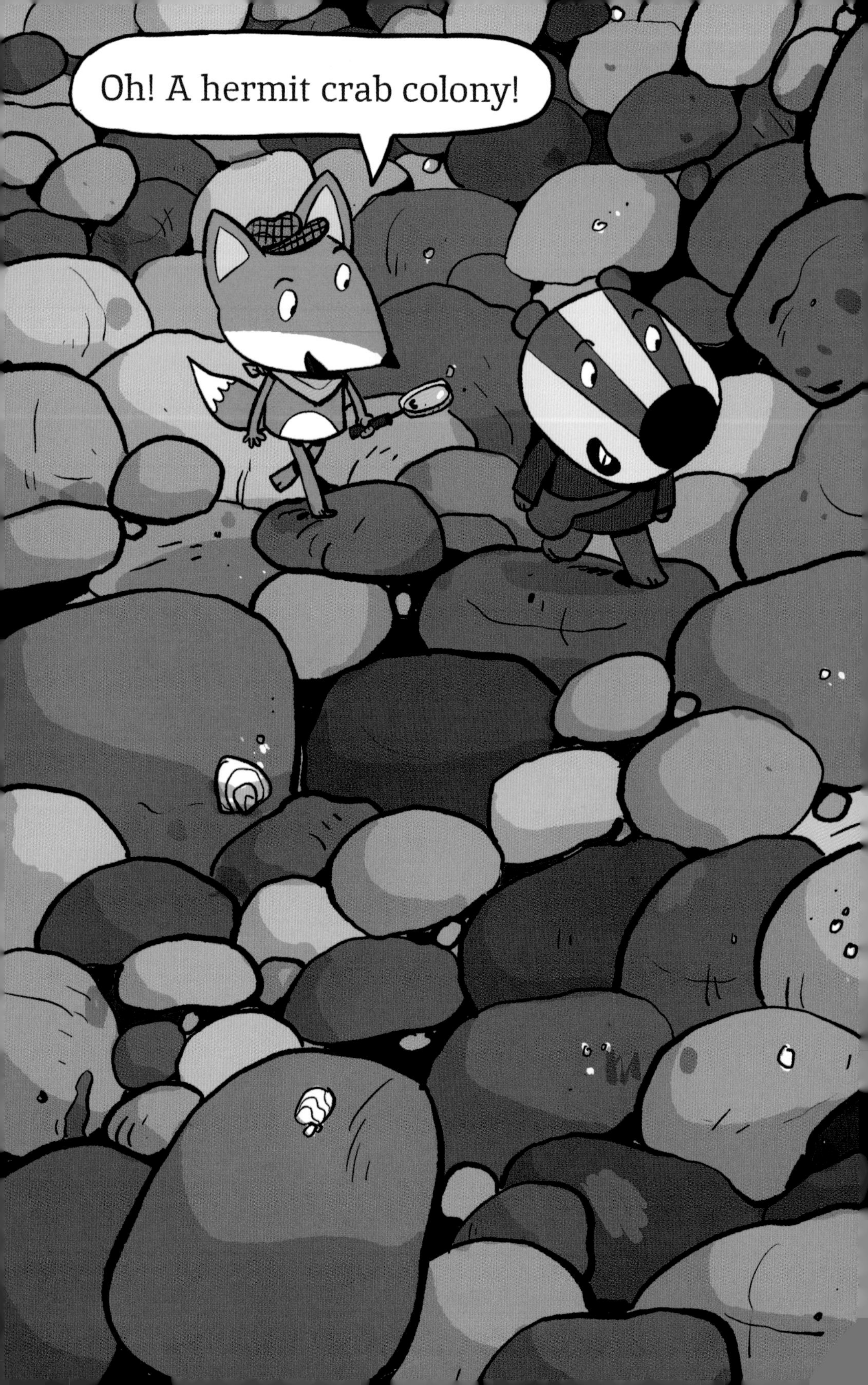
Oh! A hermit crab colony!

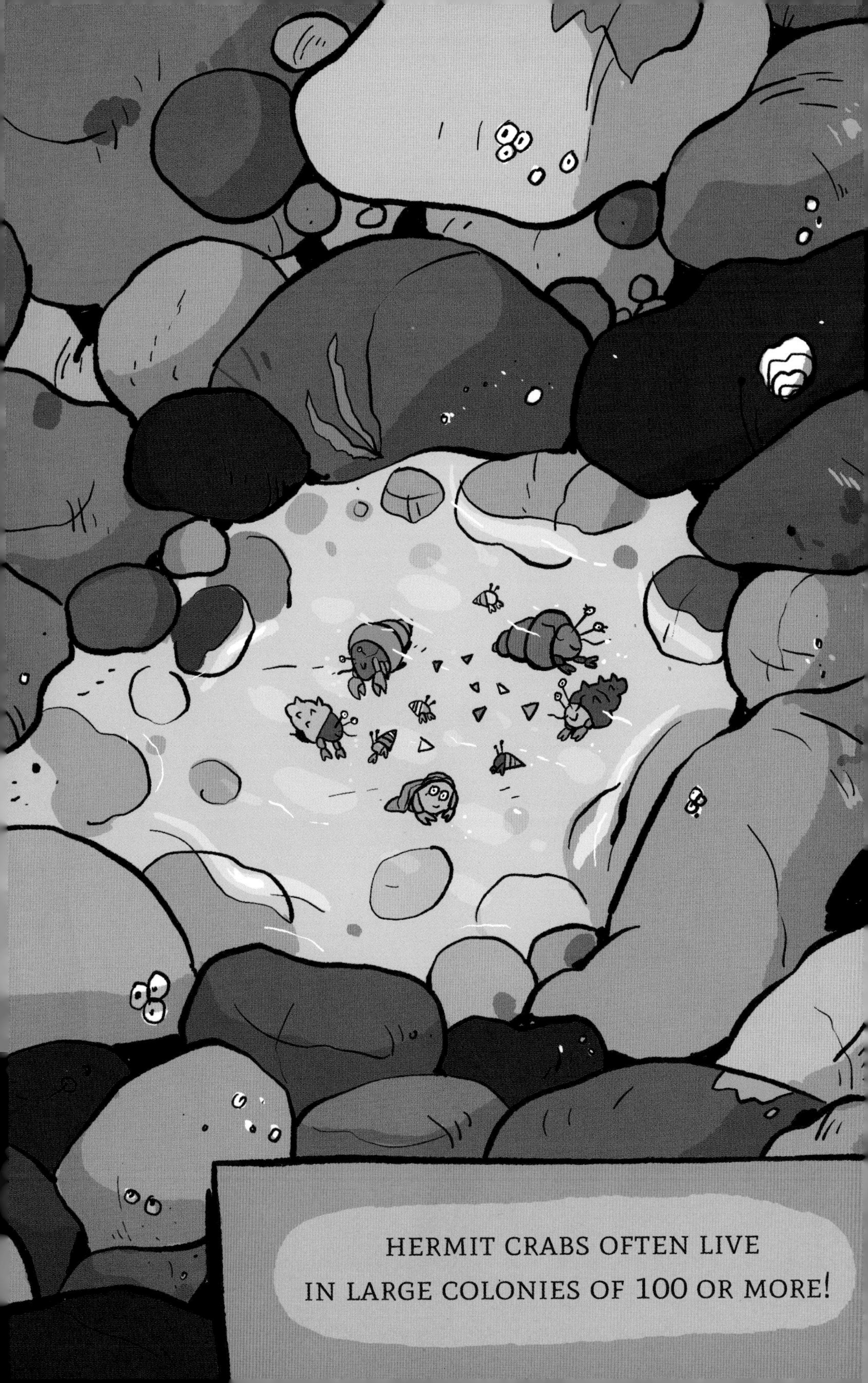
HERMIT CRABS OFTEN LIVE IN LARGE COLONIES OF 100 OR MORE!

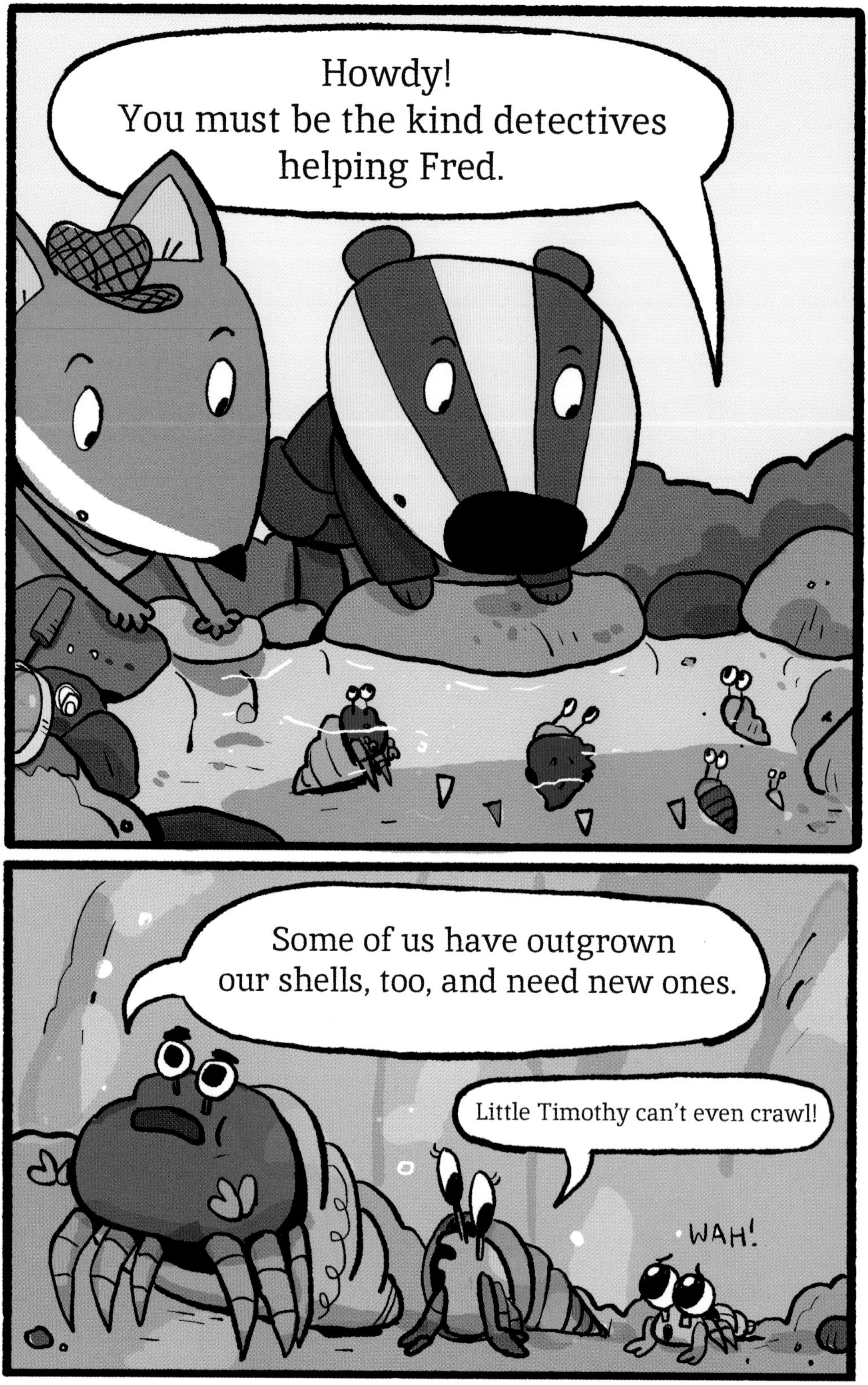
Howdy!
You must be the kind detectives helping Fred.
Some of us have outgrown our shells, too, and need new ones.
Little Timothy can't even crawl!
WAH!

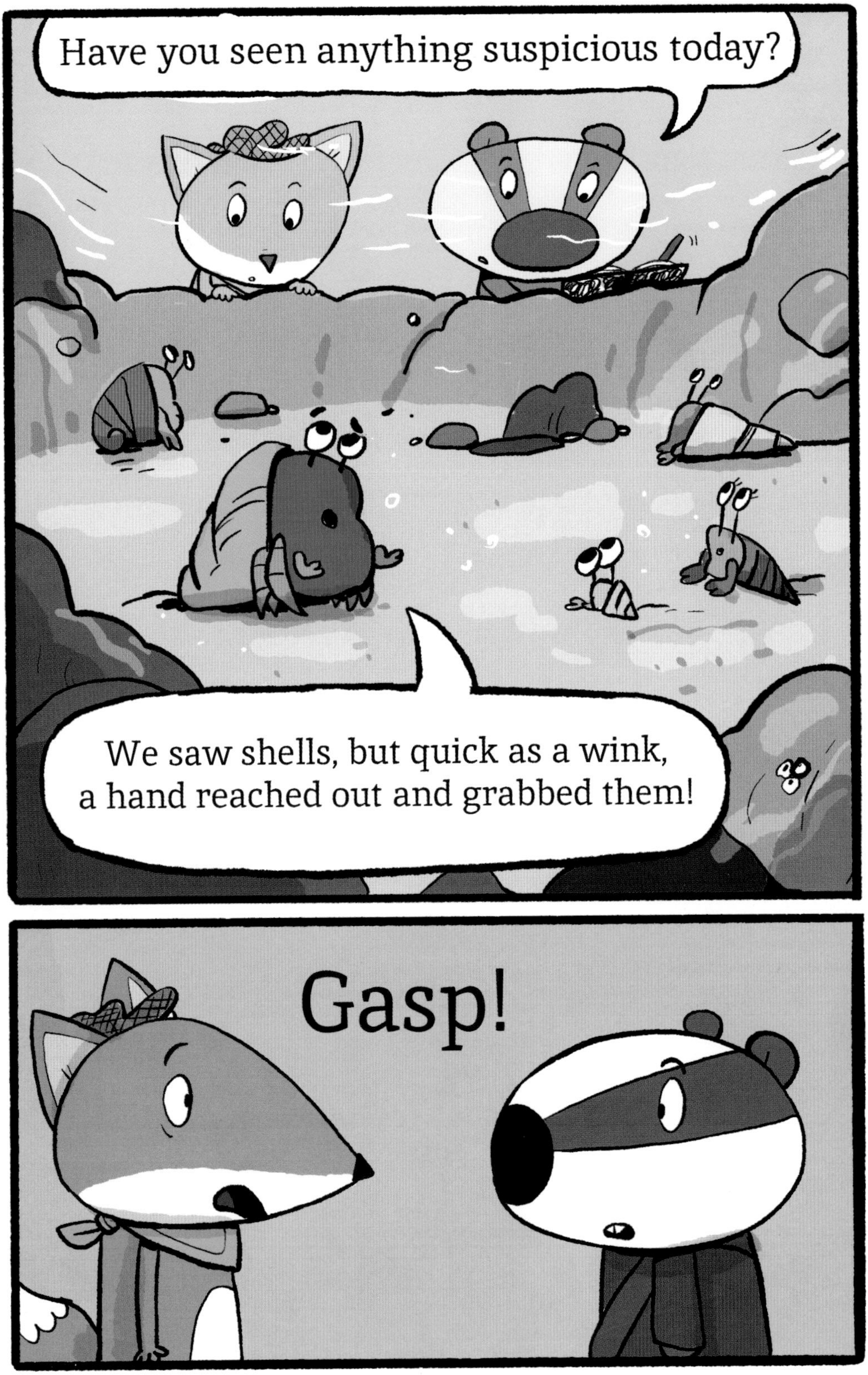
Have you seen anything suspicious today?
We saw shells, but quick as a wink, a hand reached out and grabbed them!
Gasp!

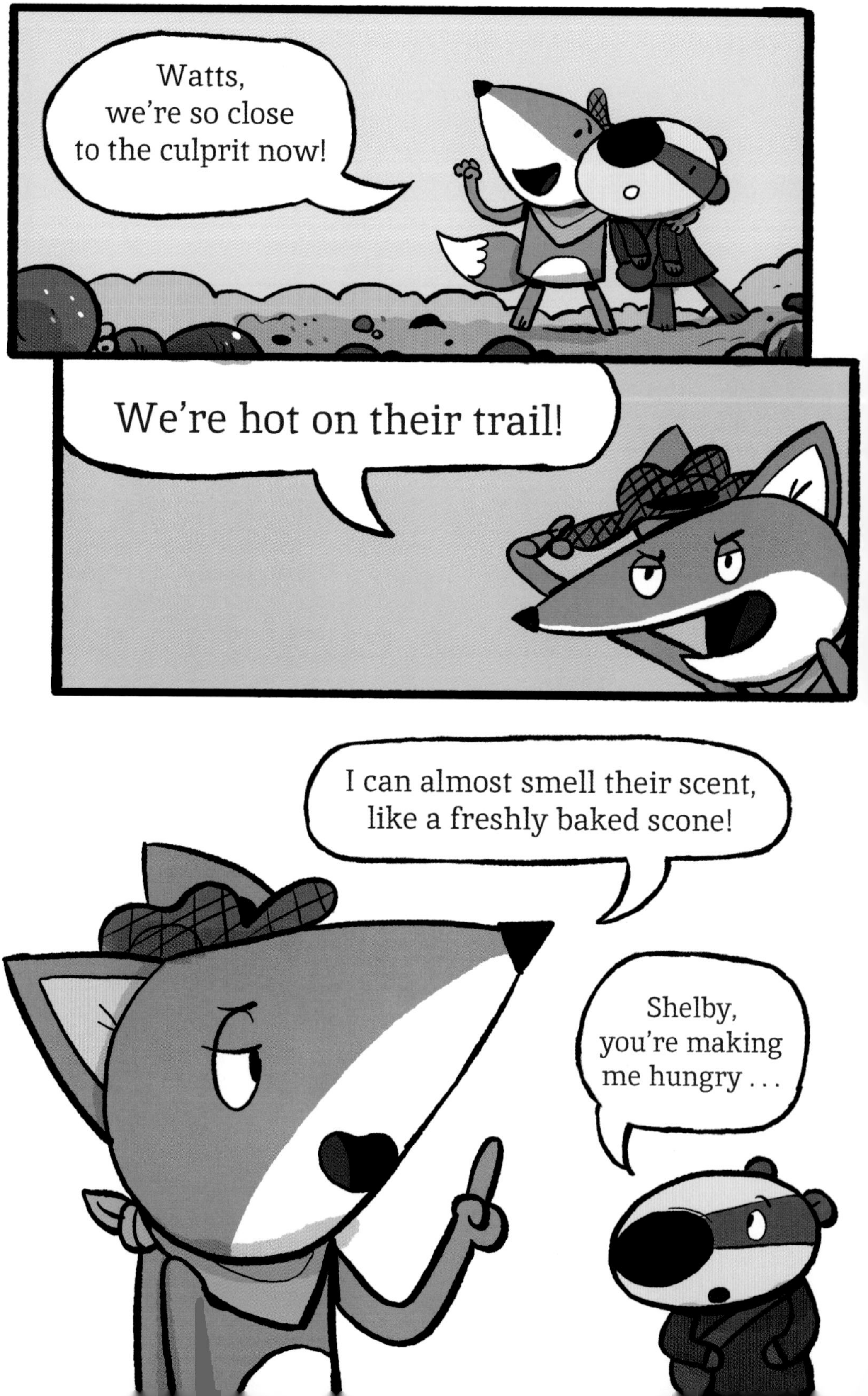
Watts,
we're so close
to the culprit now!
We're hot on their trail!
I can almost smell their scent,
like a freshly baked scone!
Shelby,
you're making
me hungry . . .

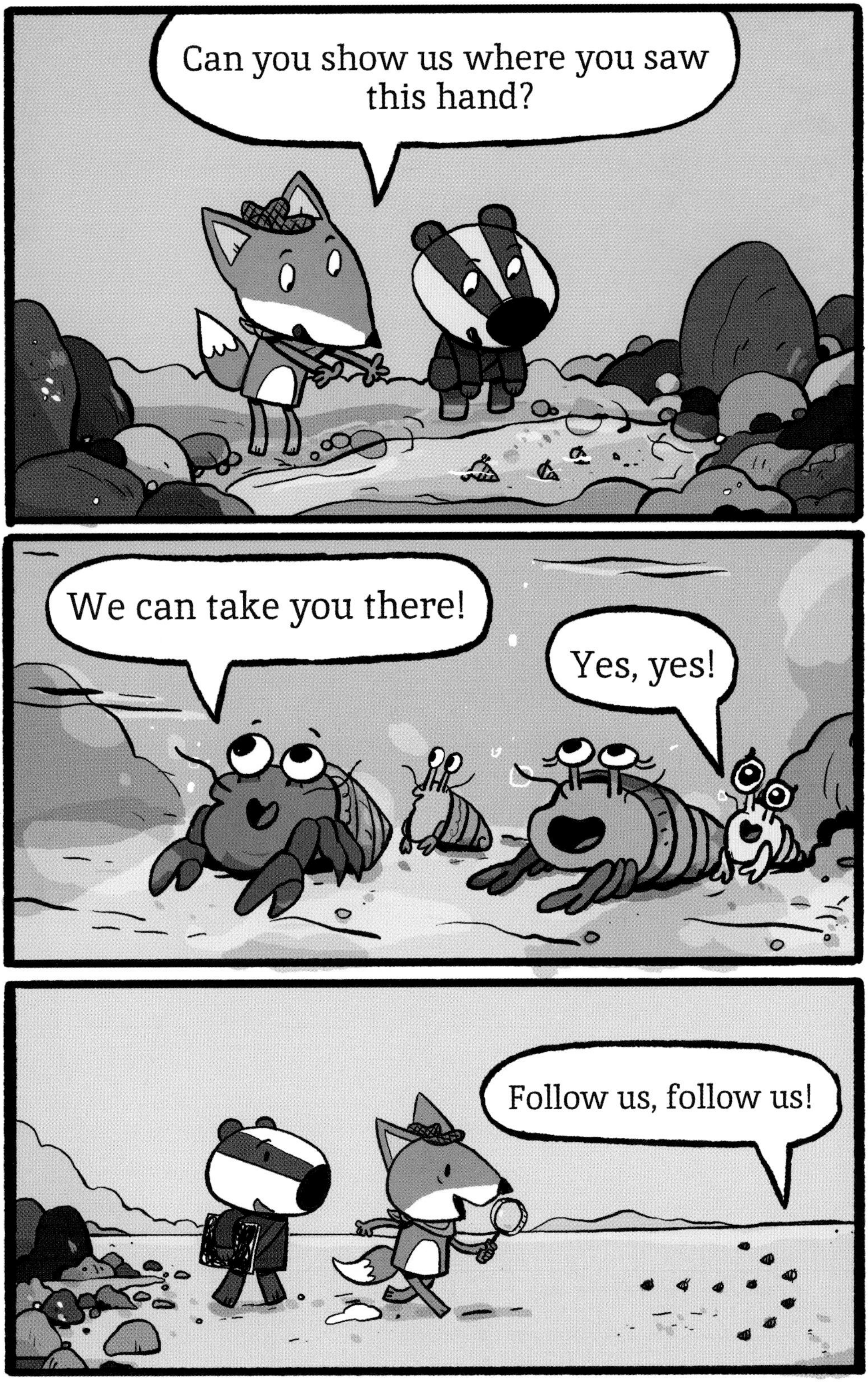
Can you show us where you saw this hand?
We can take you there!
Yes, yes!
Follow us, follow us!

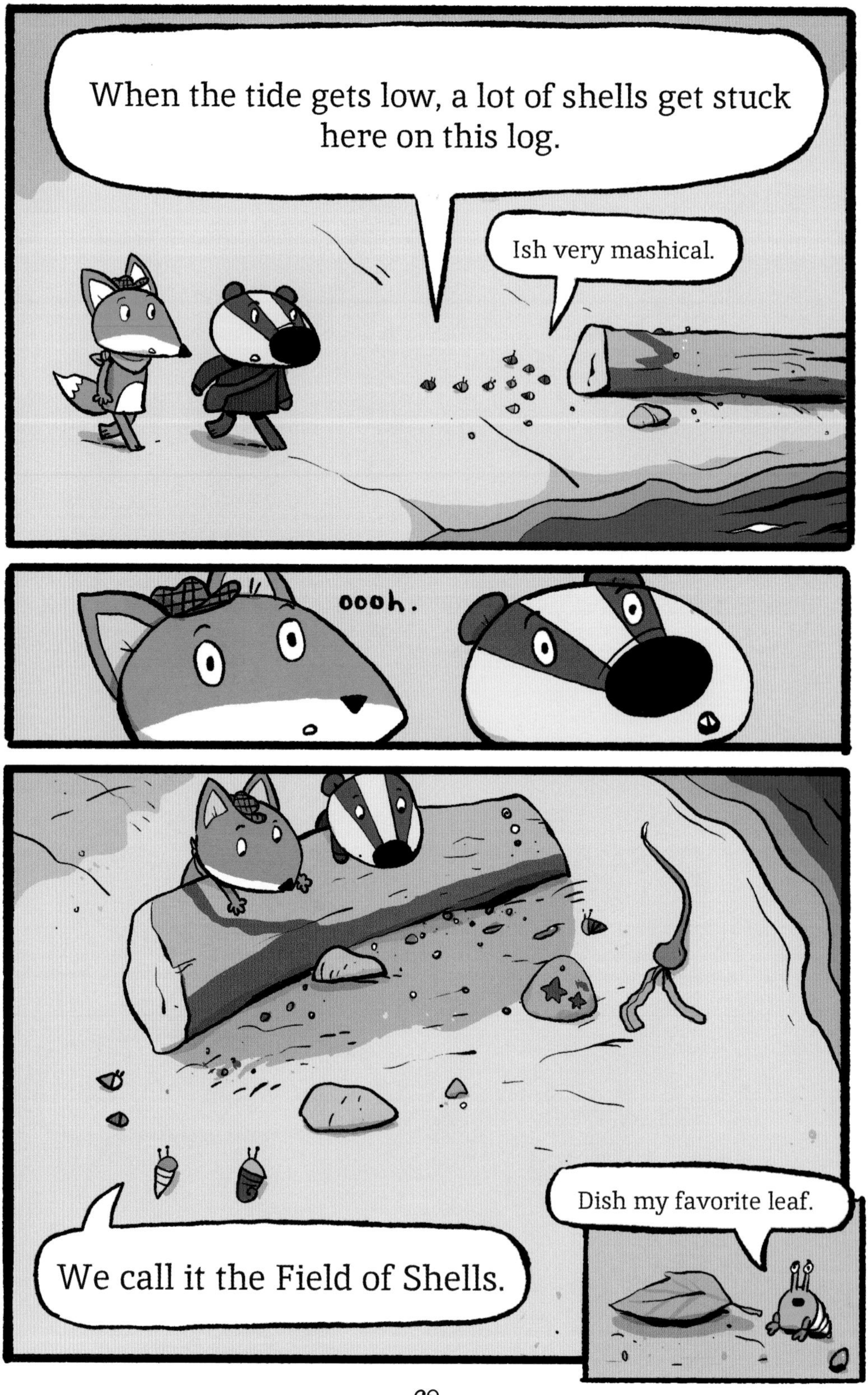
When the tide gets low, a lot of shells get stuck here on this log.
Ish very mashical.
oooh.
We call it the Field of Shells.
Dish my favorite leaf.

CHAPTER 5

At the Field of Shells . . .

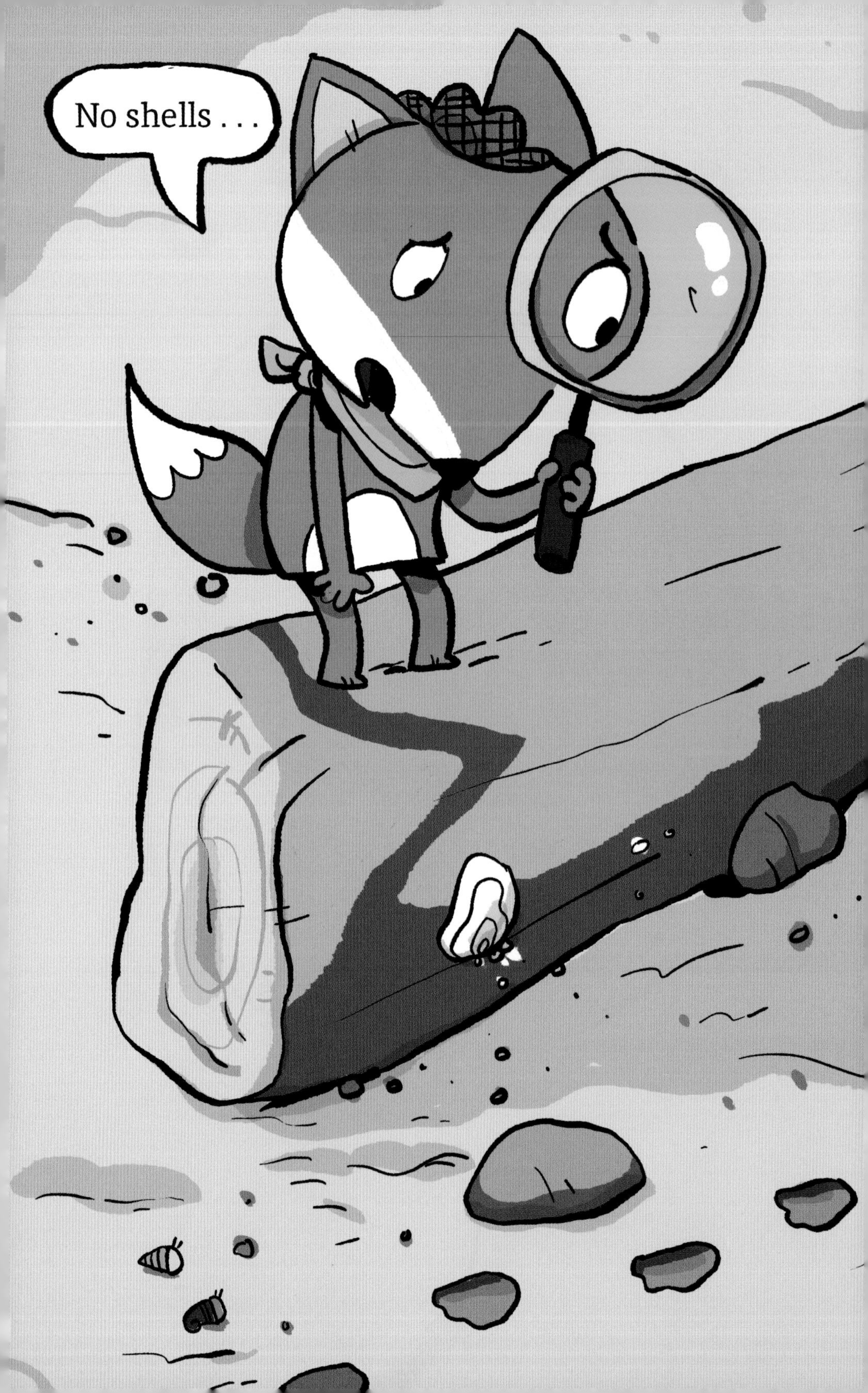
No shells . . .

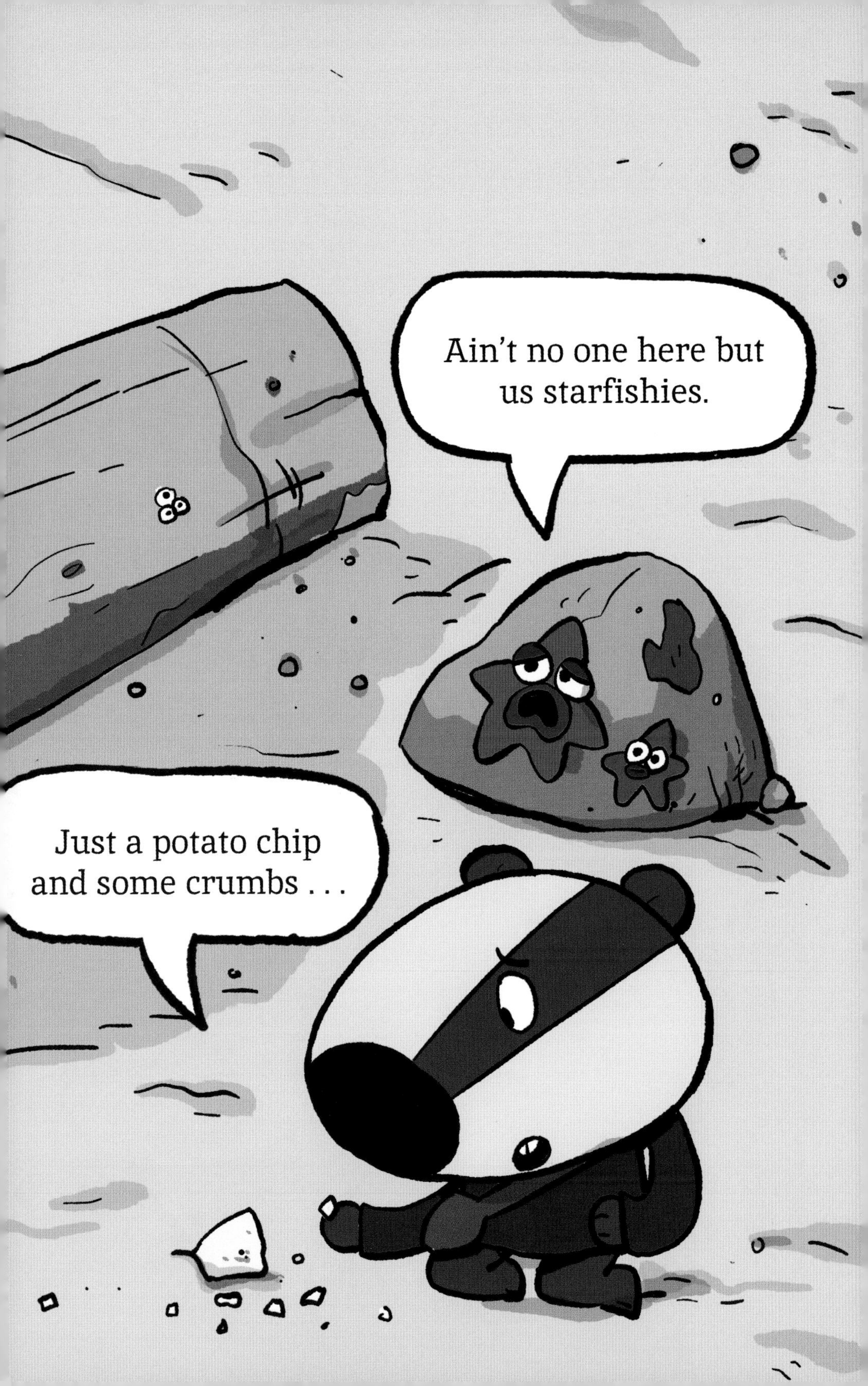
Ain't no one here but us starfishies.
Just a potato chip and some crumbs . . .

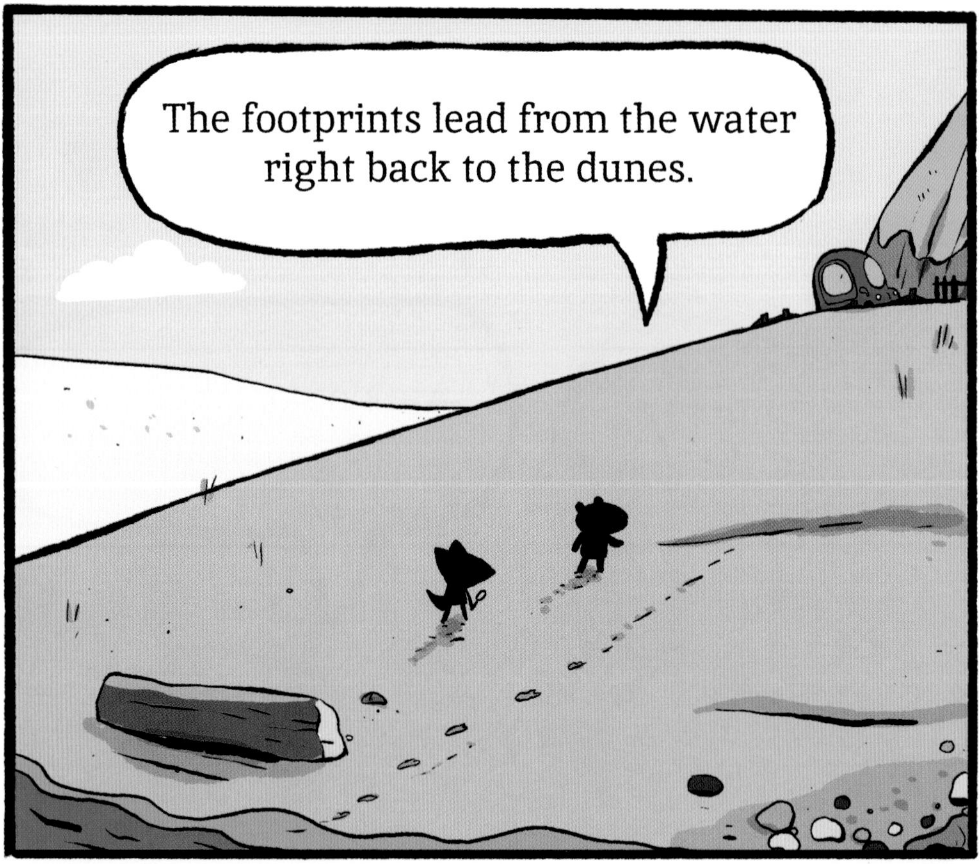
The footprints lead from the water right back to the dunes.

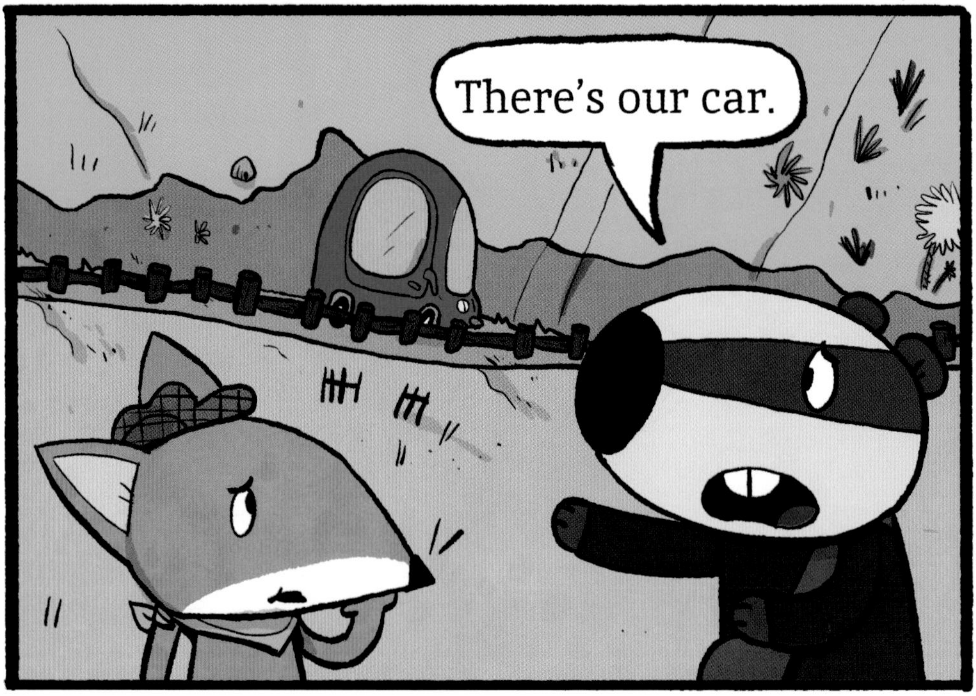
There's our car.

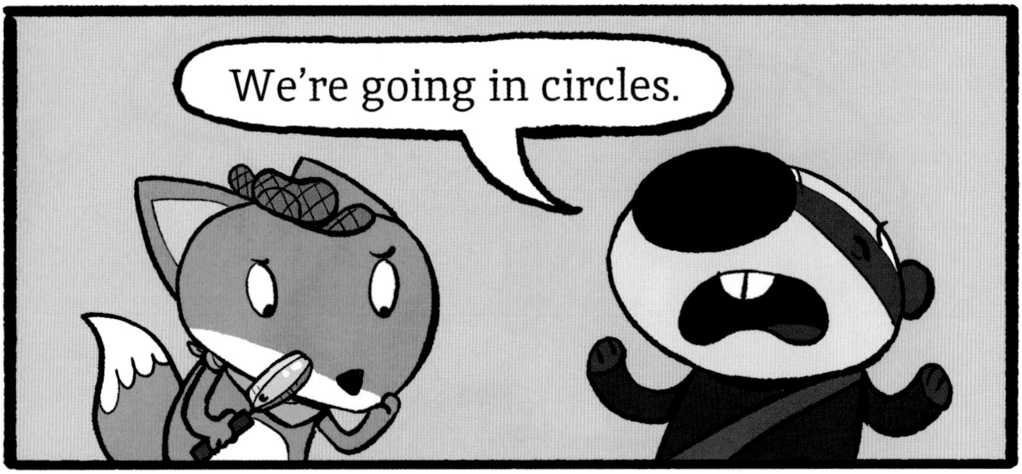
We're going in circles.

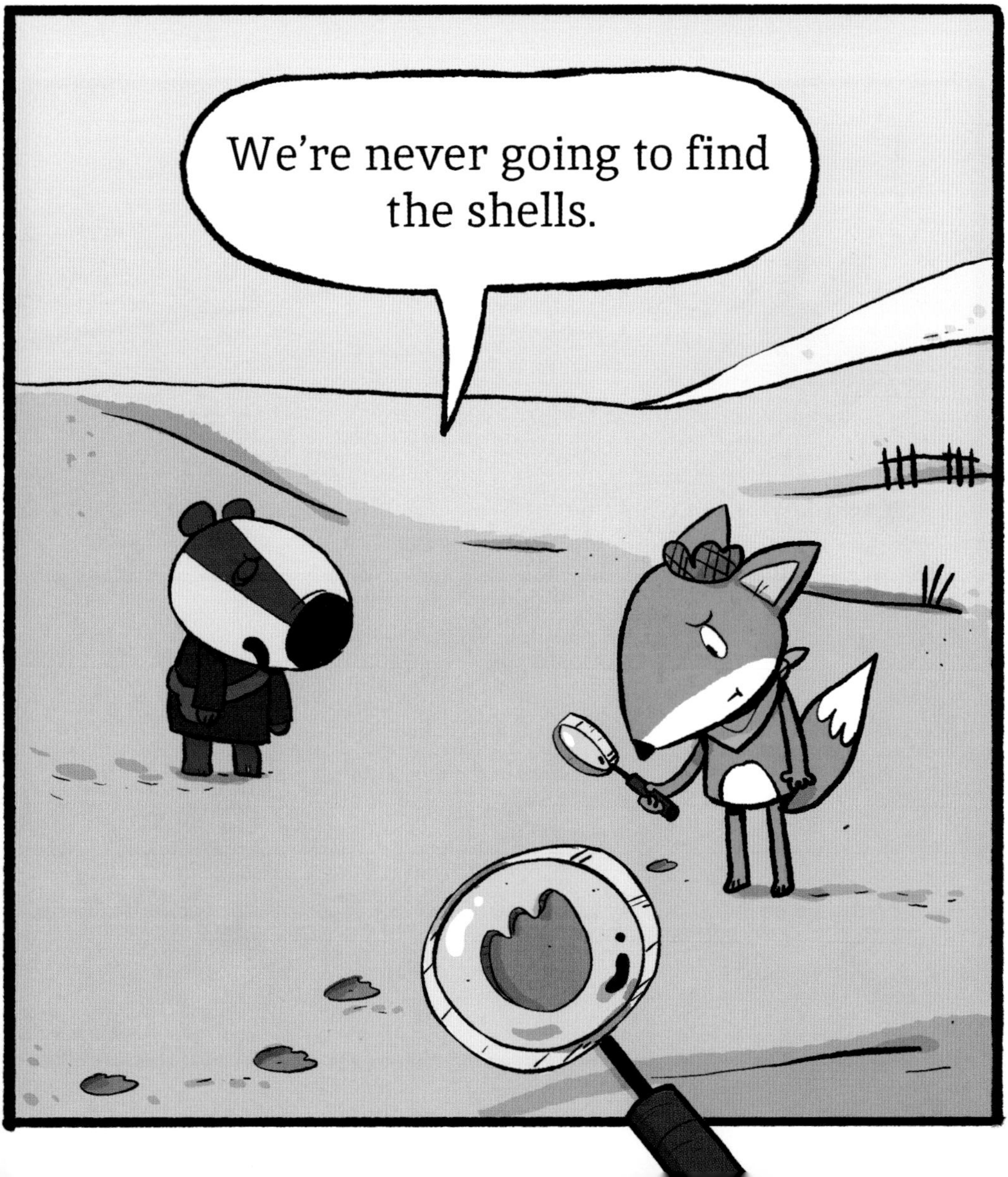
We're never going to find the shells.

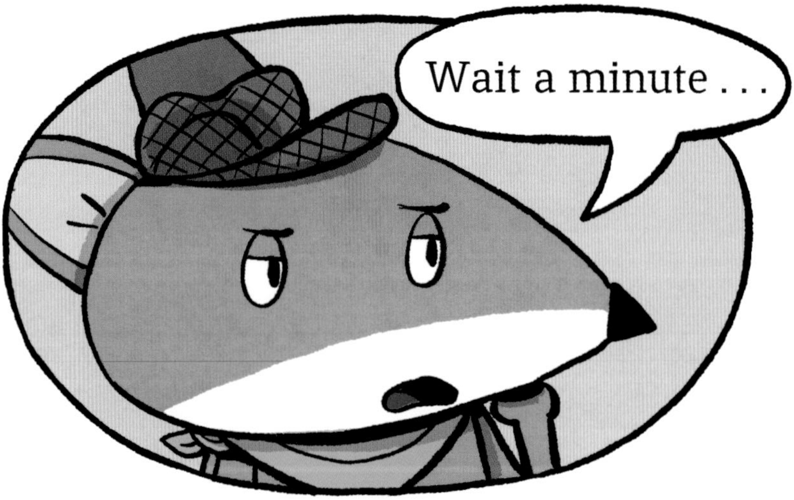
Wait a minute . . .

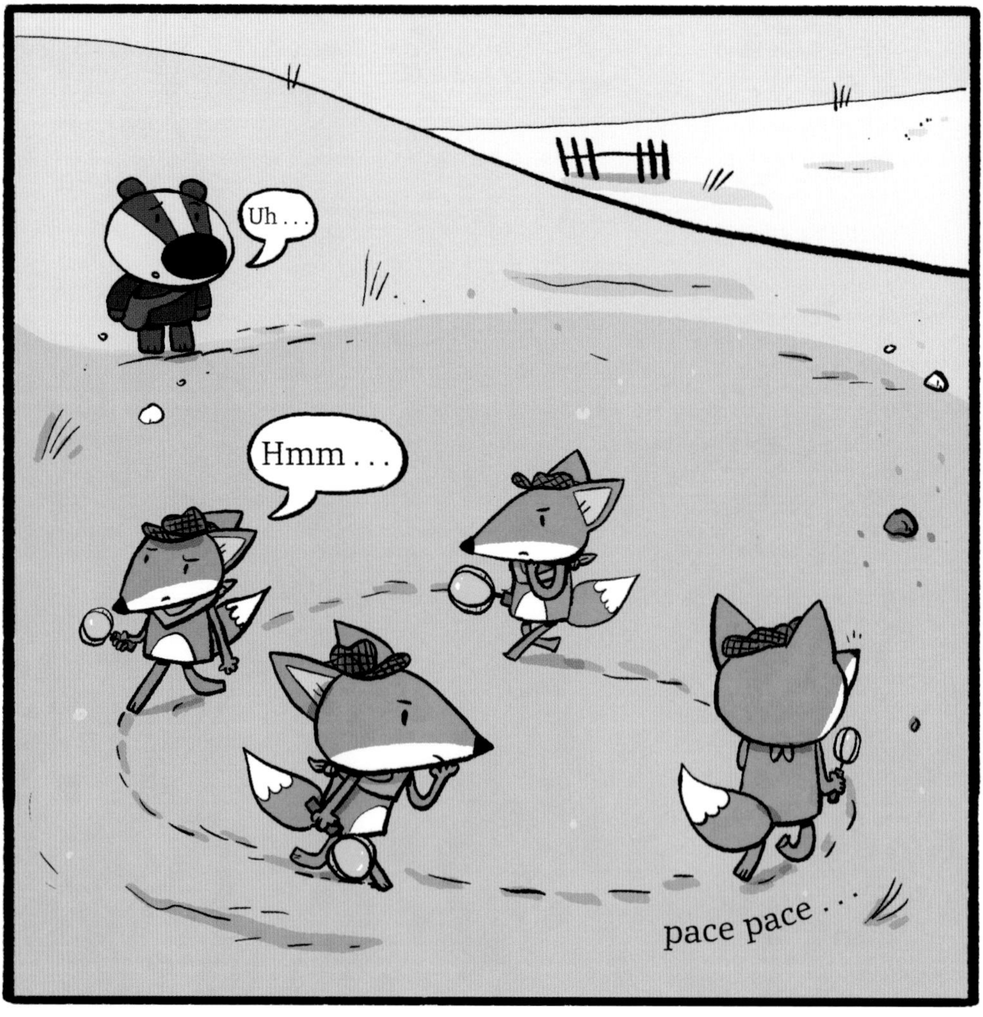
Uh . . .
Hmm . . .
pace pace . . .

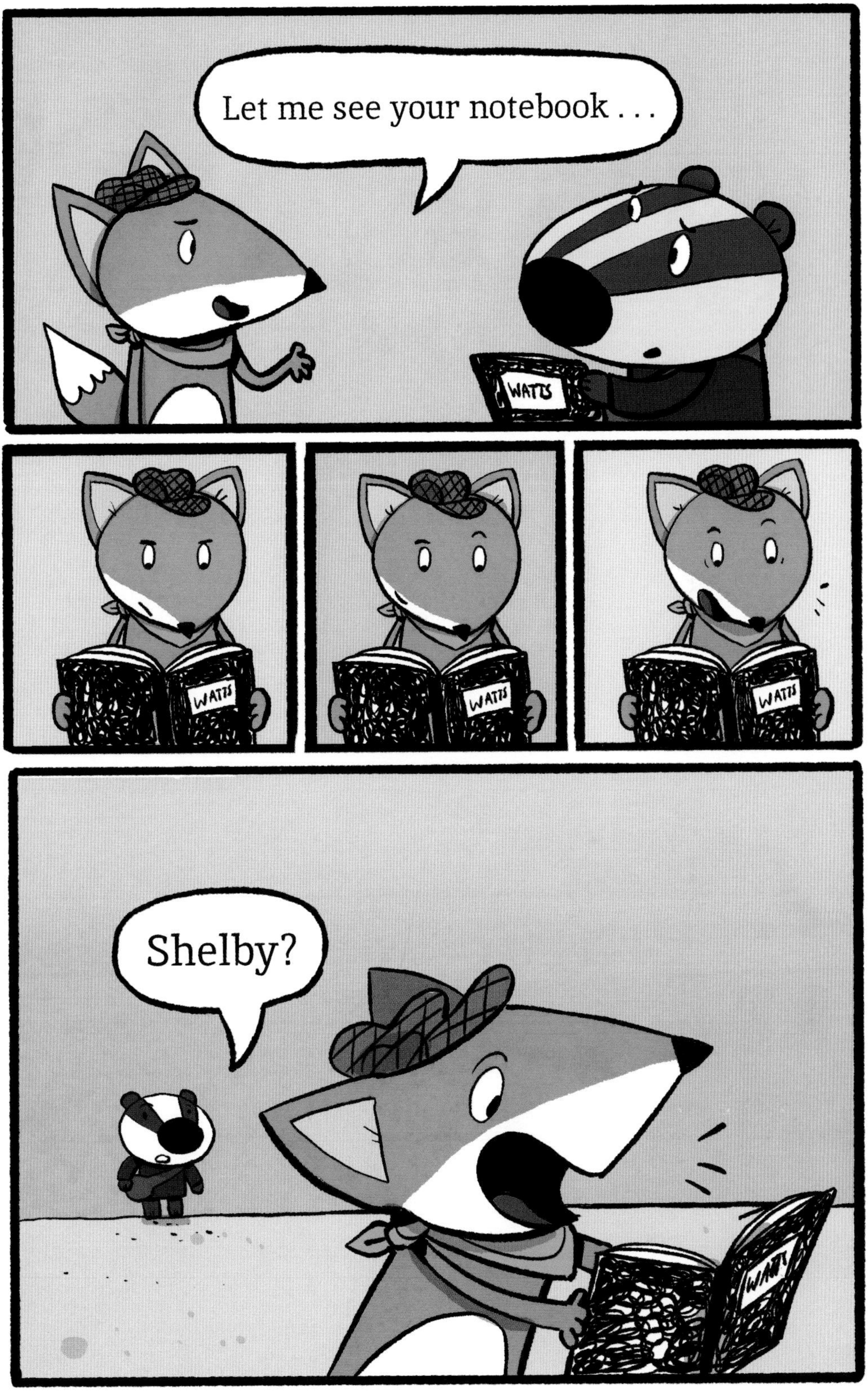
Let me see your notebook . . .
WATTS
WATTS
WATTS
WATTS
Shelby?
WATTS

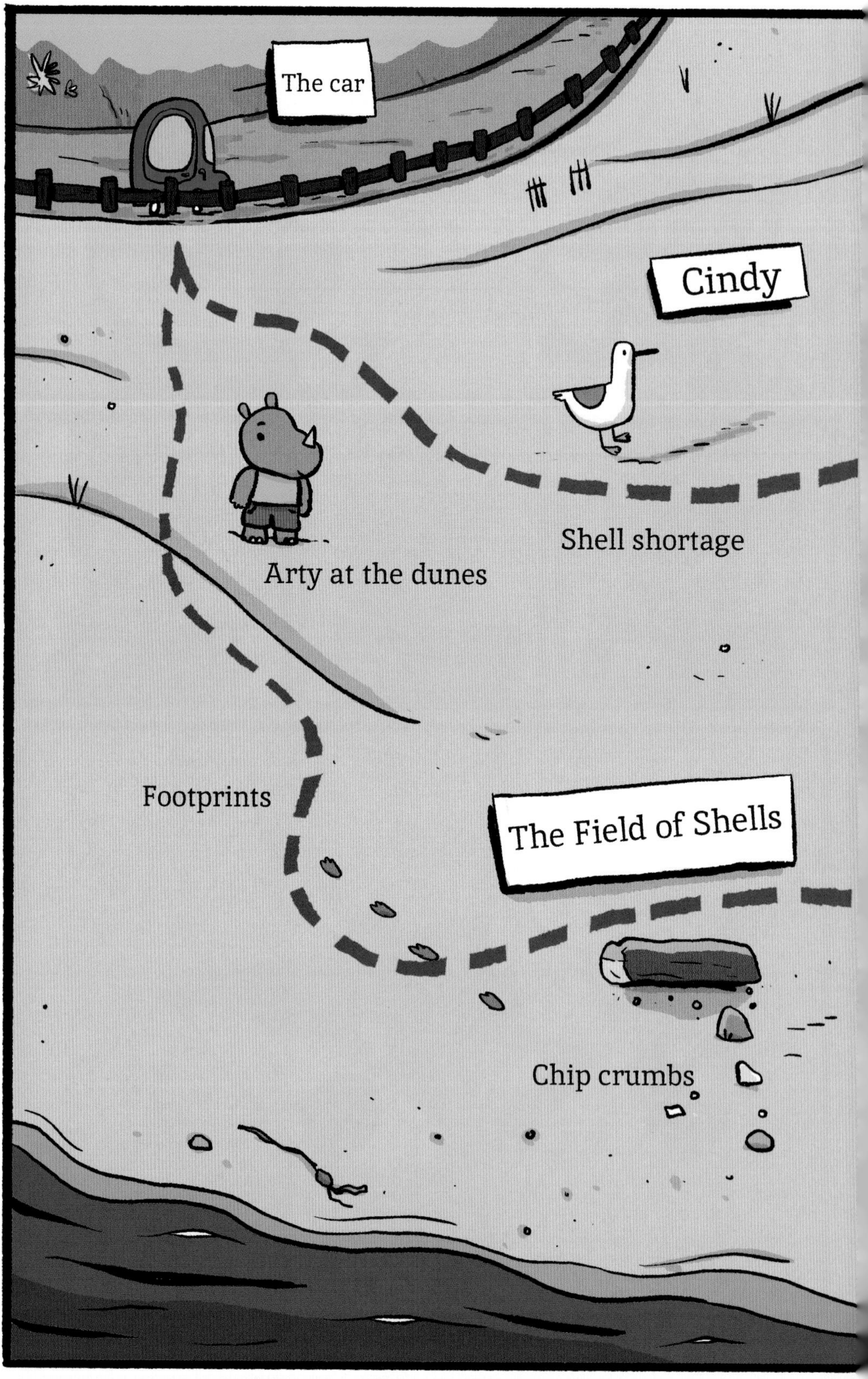
The car
Cindy
Shell shortage
Arty at the dunes
Footprints
The Field of Shells
Chip crumbs

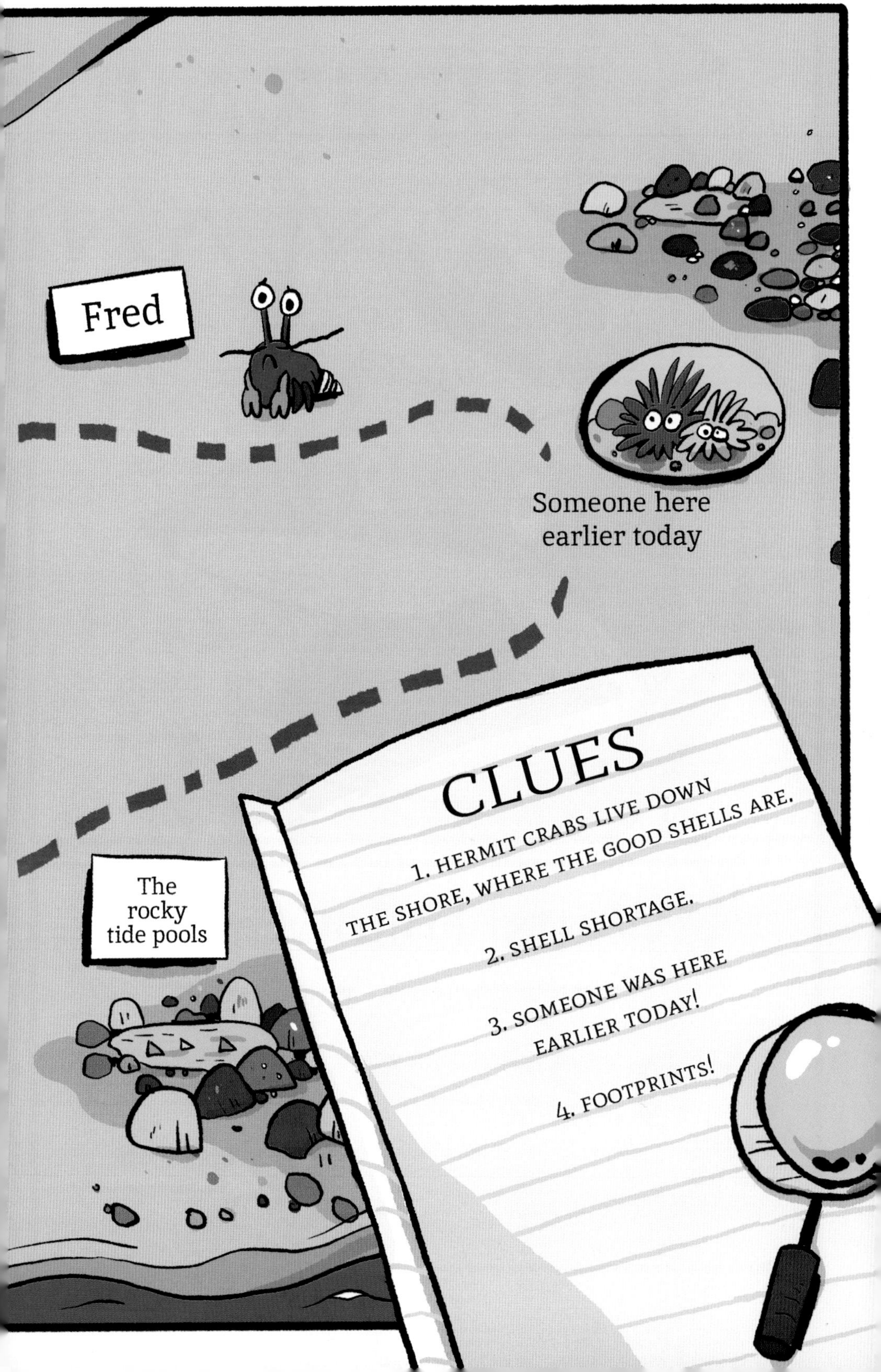
Fred
Someone here earlier today
The rocky tide pools
CLUES
1. HERMIT CRABS LIVE DOWN THE SHORE, WHERE THE GOOD SHELLS ARE.
2. SHELL SHORTAGE.
3. SOMEONE WAS HERE EARLIER TODAY!
4. FOOTPRINTS!

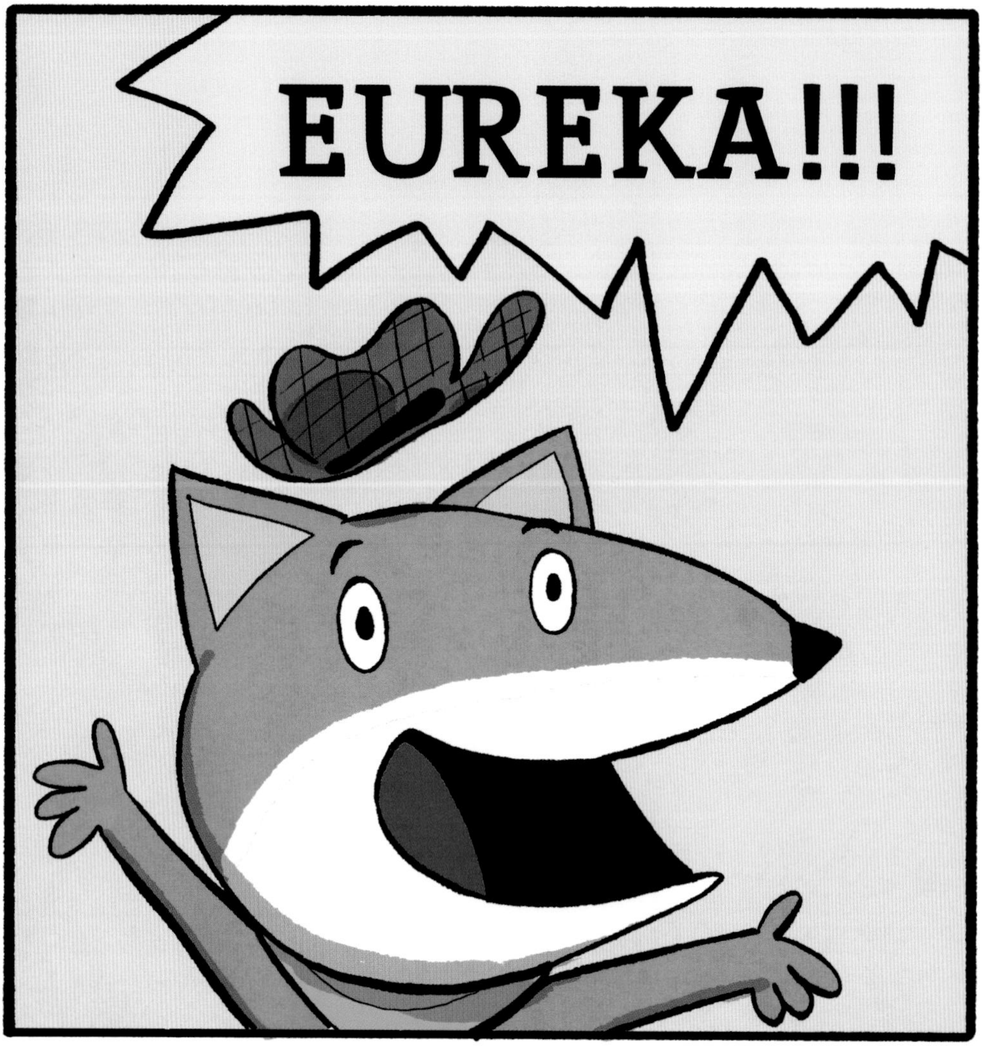
EUREKA!!!

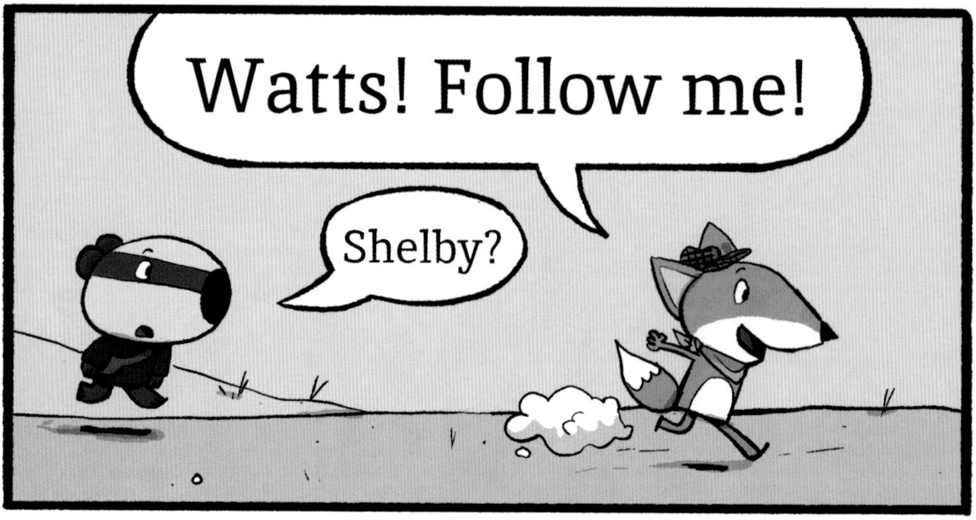
Watts! Follow me!
Shelby?

CHAPTER 6

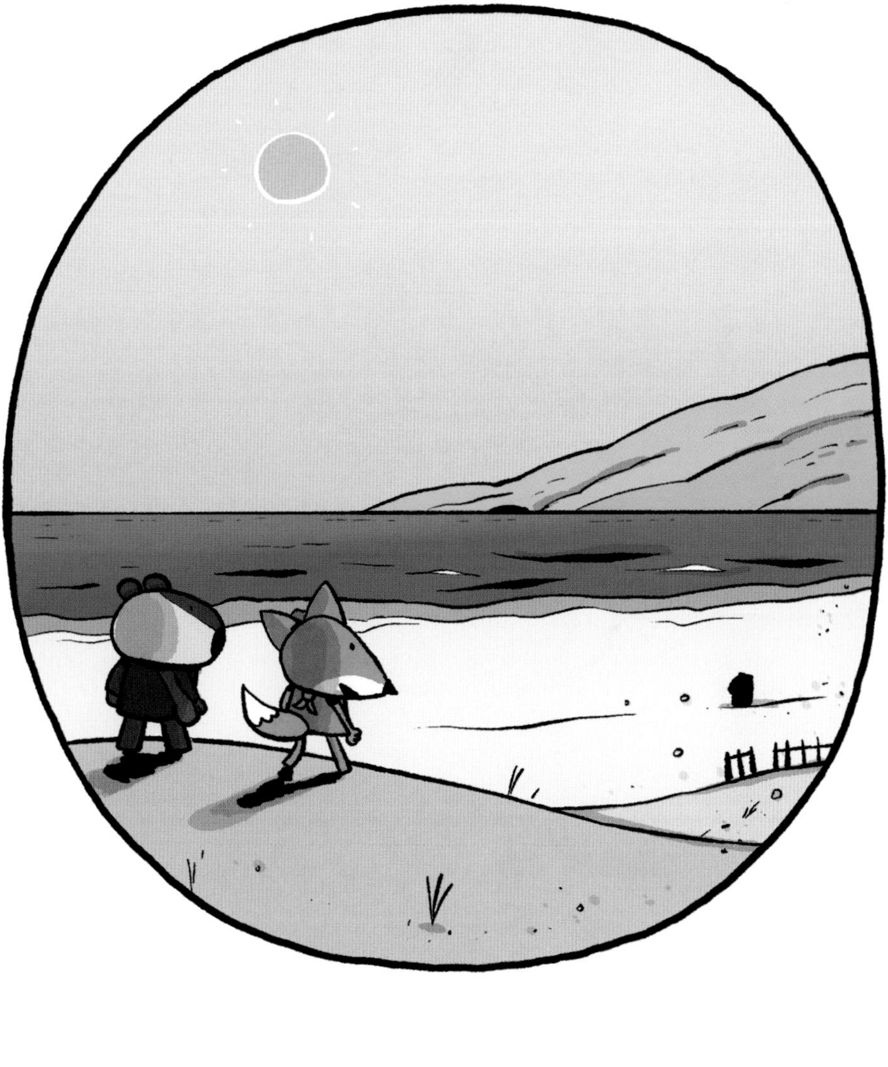

The beach dunes . . .

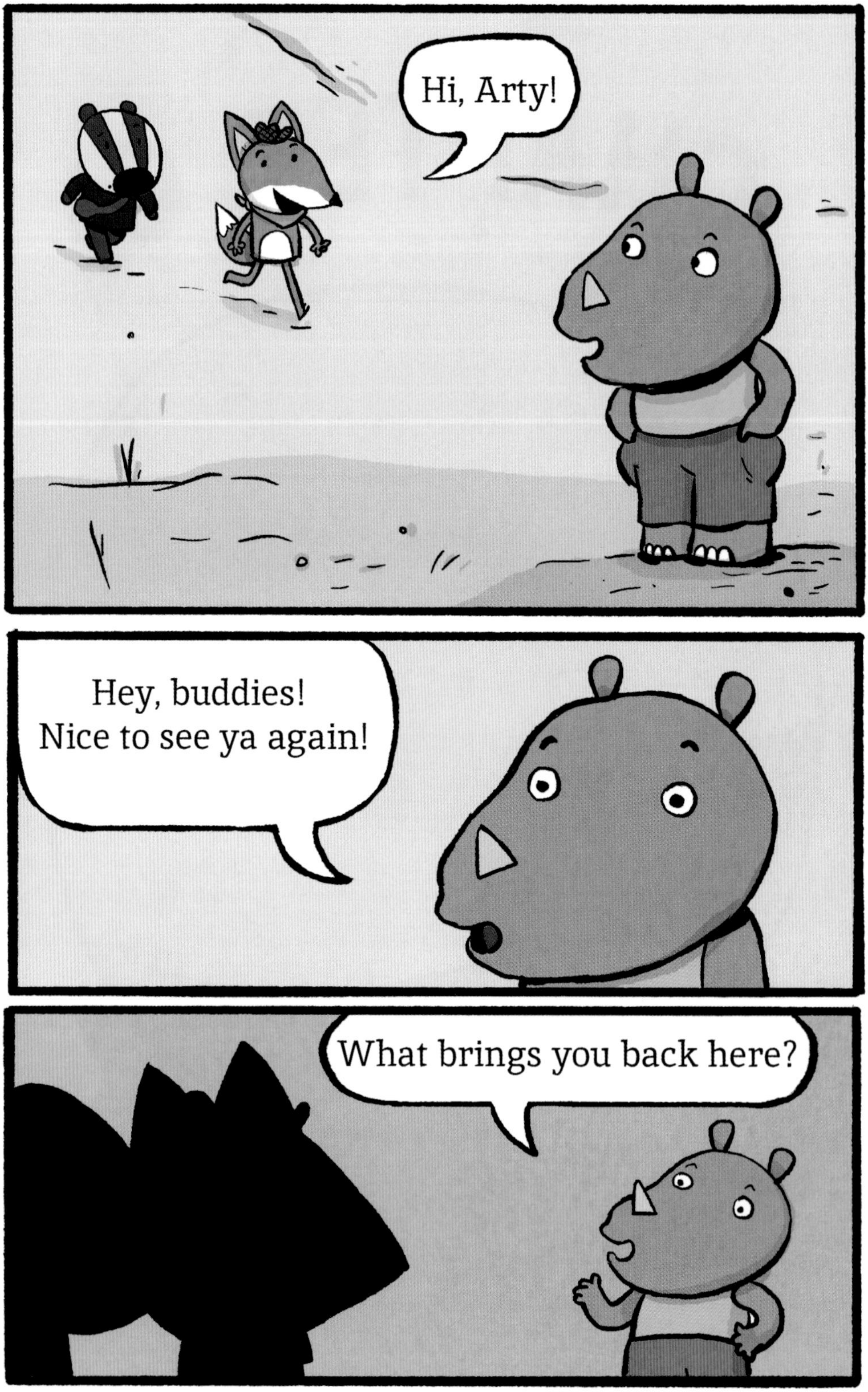
Hi, Arty!
Hey, buddies! Nice to see ya again!
What brings you back here?

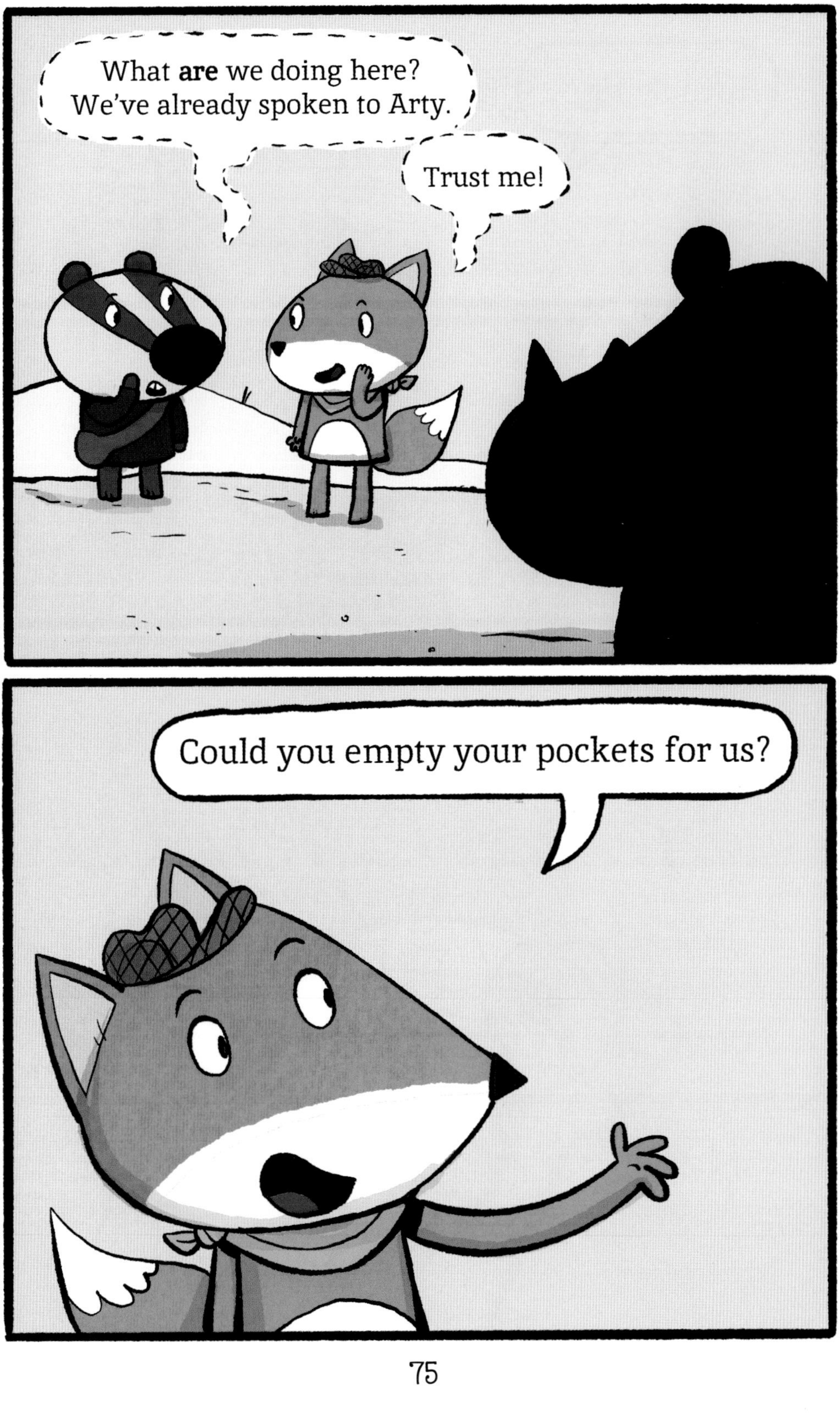
What **are** we doing here? We've already spoken to Arty.
Trust me!
Could you empty your pockets for us?

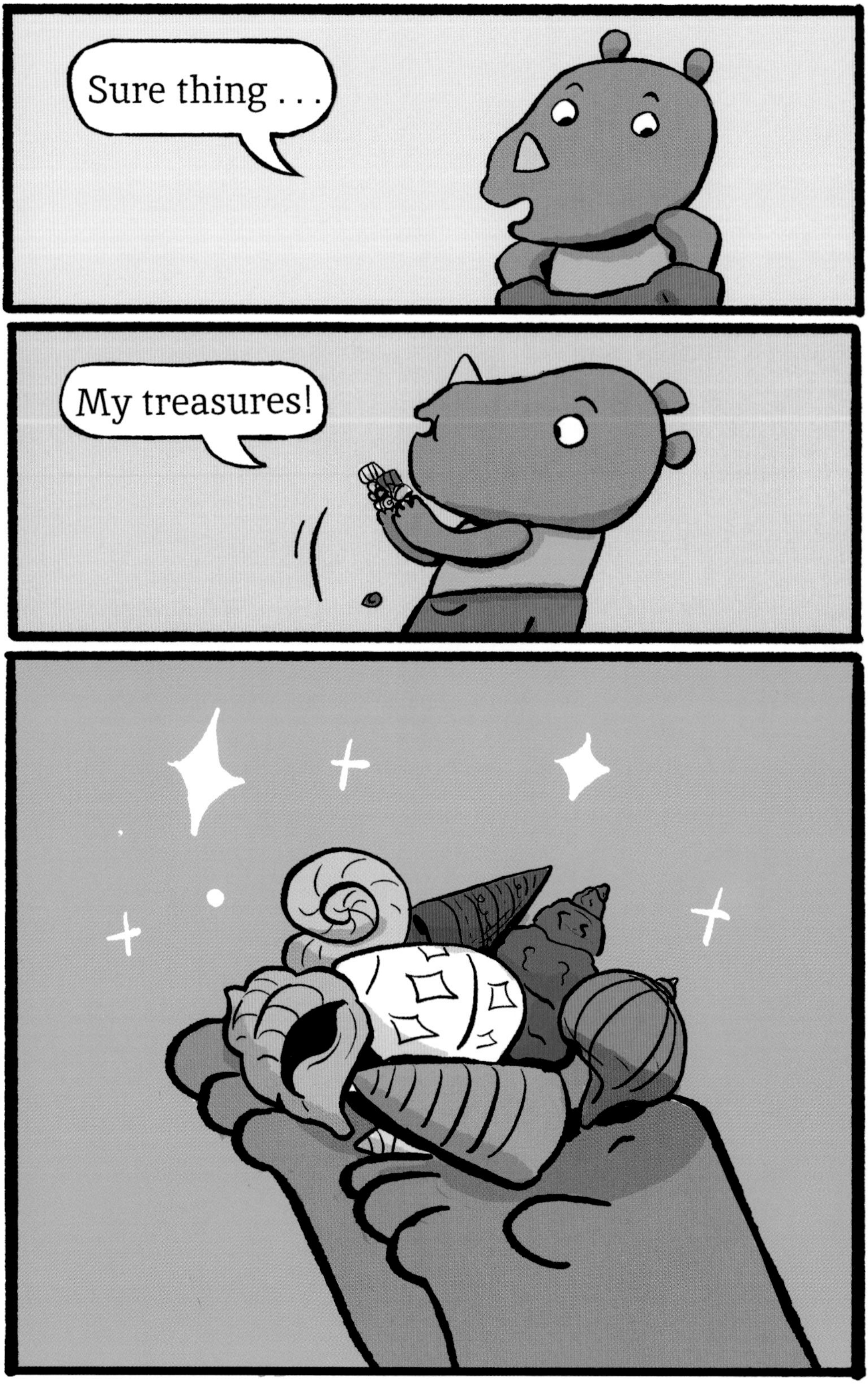
Sure thing . . .
My treasures!

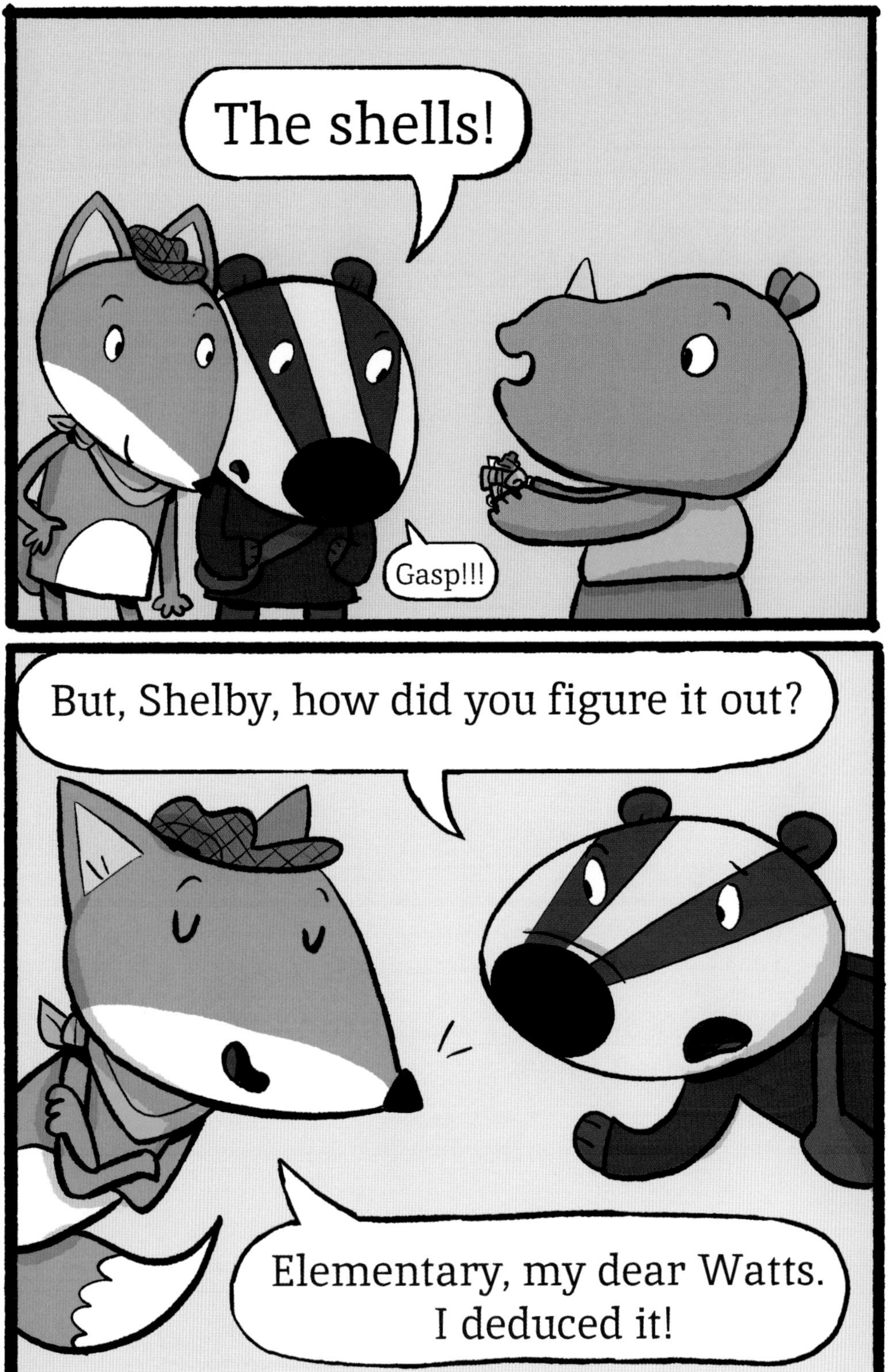
The shells!
Gasp!!!
But, Shelby, how did you figure it out?
Elementary, my dear Watts.
I deduced it!

The Case of the Missing Shells

Clue: Arty was eating chips, which we later found at the shore.

Arty: seaside collector

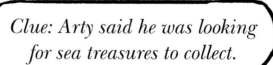

Clue: Arty said he was looking for sea treasures to collect.

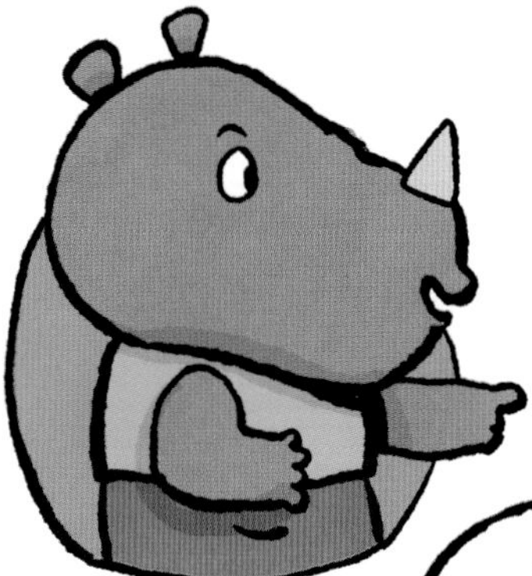

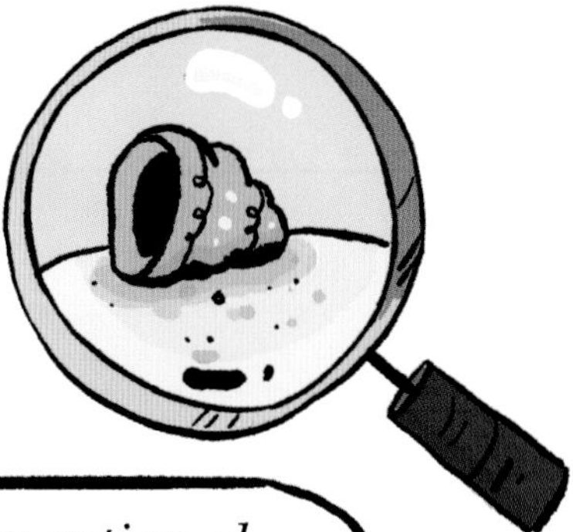

Clue: Arty mentioned "where the good shells are," which meant he often looked for shells!

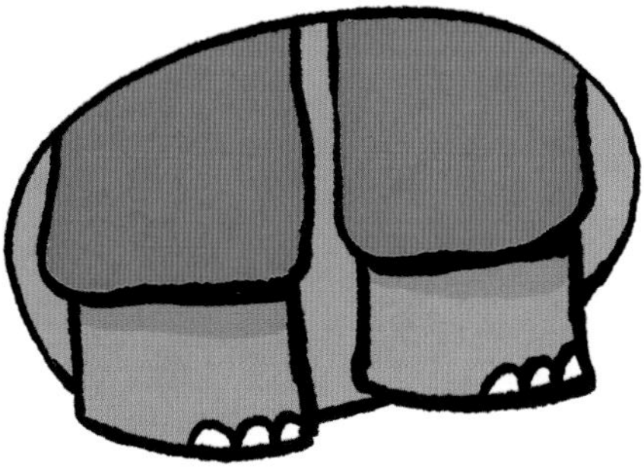

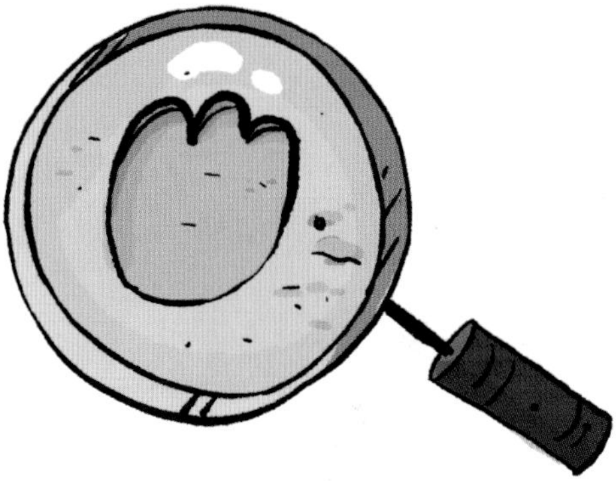

Clue: Wet footprints led from the water to the dunes . . . Rhinocerous-shaped footprints!

Solution: Arty took the shells!

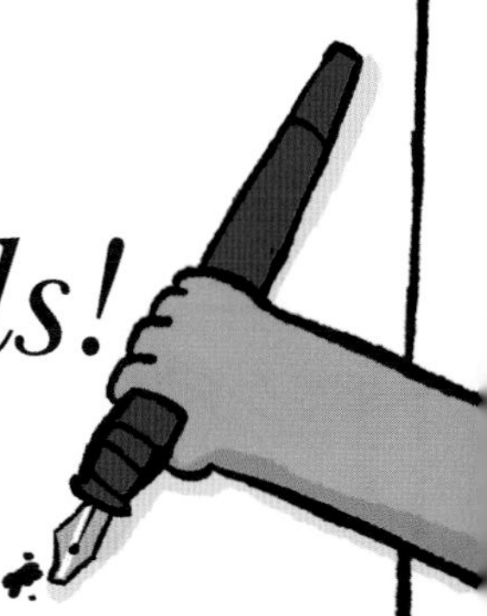

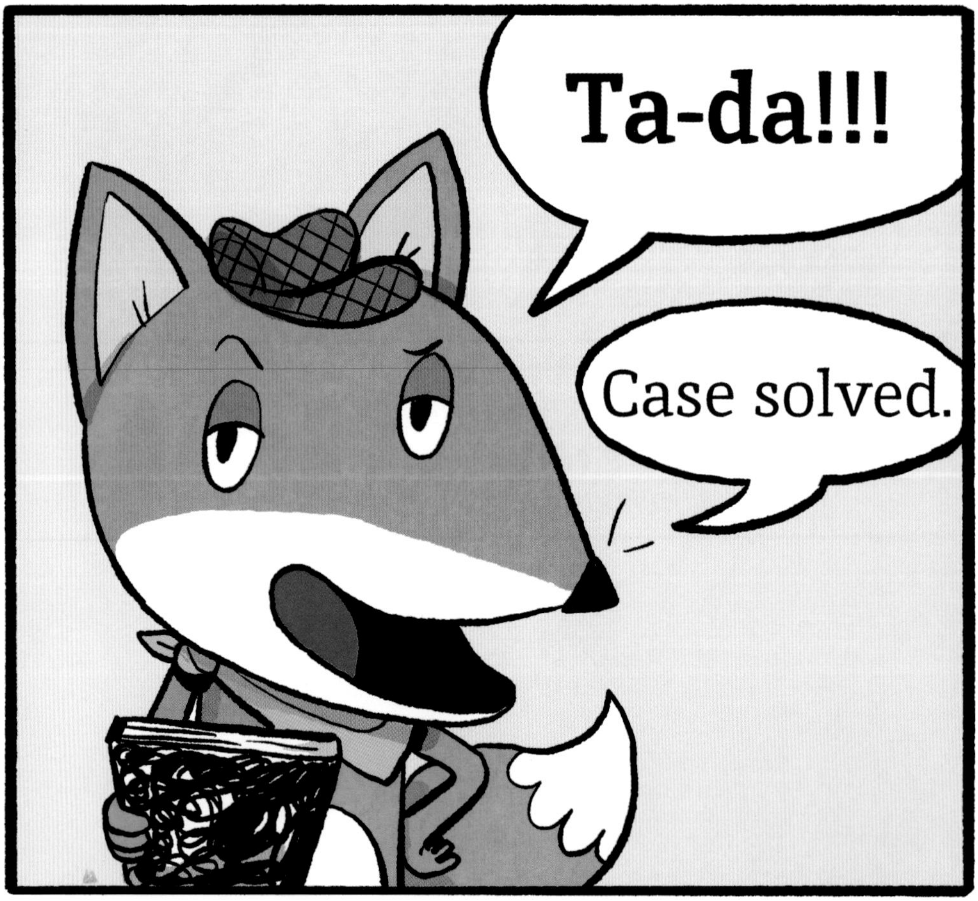
Ta-da!!!
Case solved.

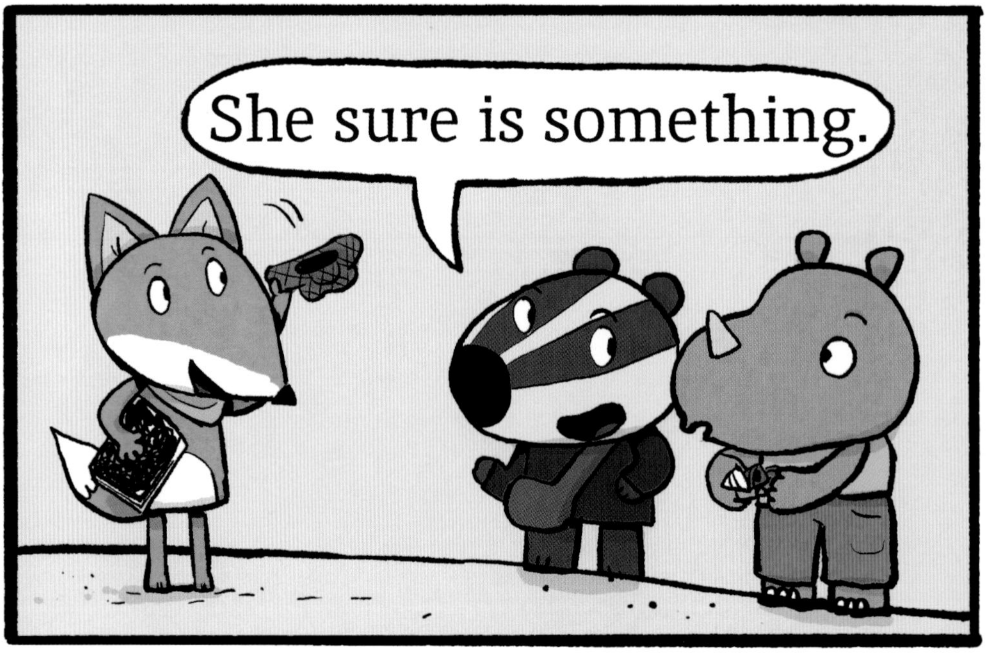
She sure is something.

CHAPTER 7

At the beach . . .

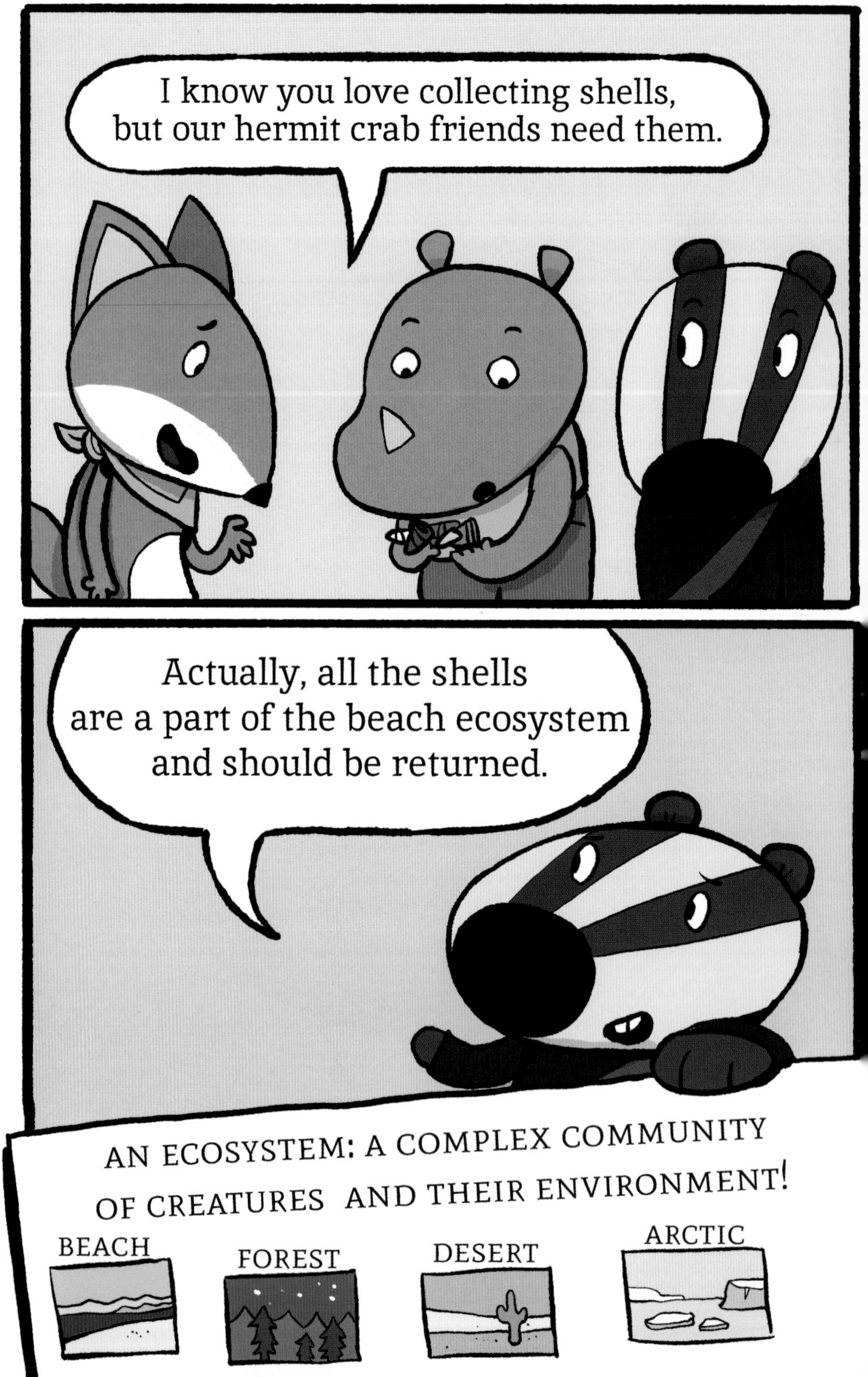
I know you love collecting shells, but our hermit crab friends need them.
Actually, all the shells are a part of the beach ecosystem and should be returned.
AN ECOSYSTEM: A COMPLEX COMMUNITY OF CREATURES AND THEIR ENVIRONMENT!
BEACH
FOREST
DESERT
ARCTIC

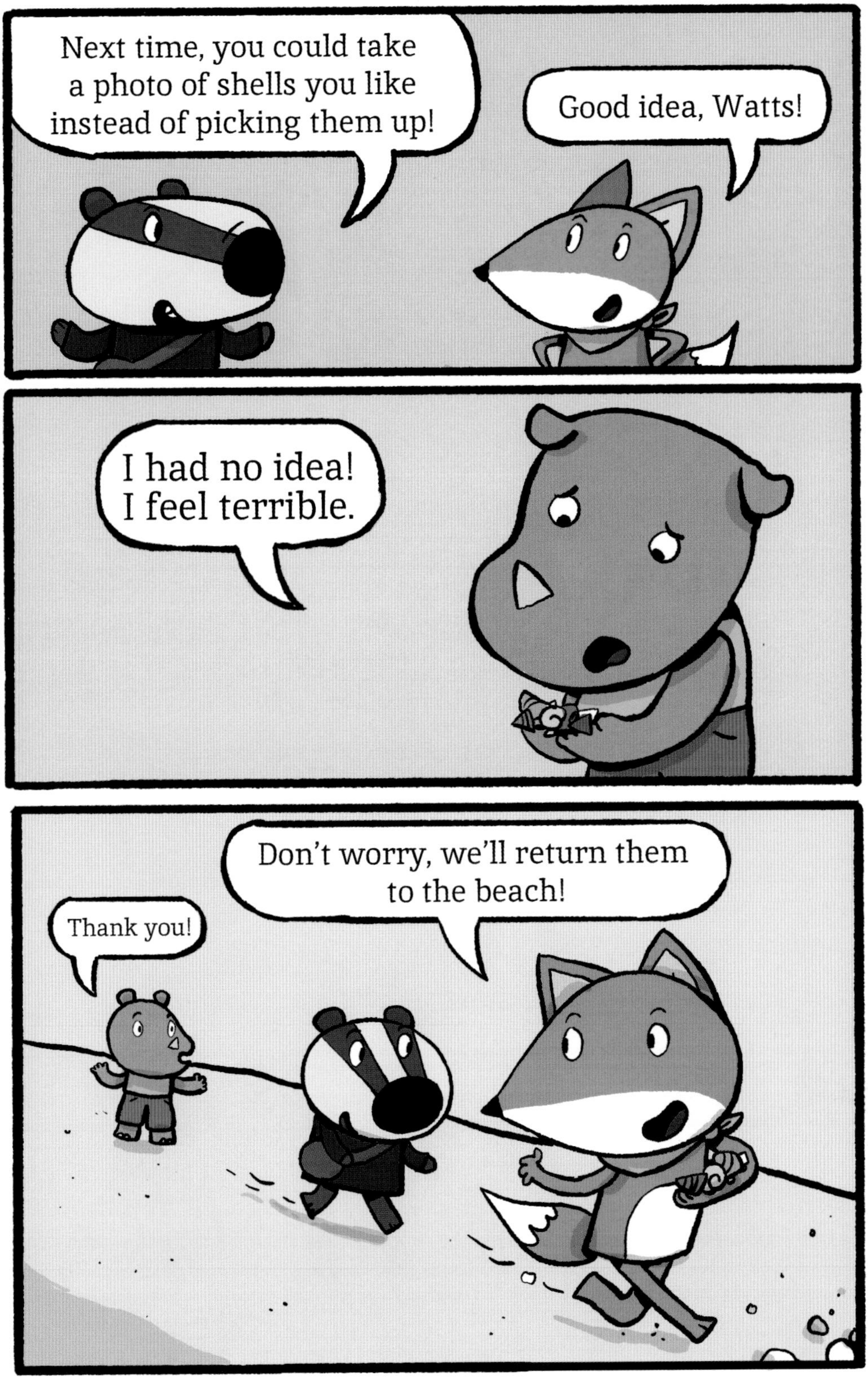
Next time, you could take a photo of shells you like instead of picking them up!
Good idea, Watts!
I had no idea! I feel terrible.
Thank you!
Don't worry, we'll return them to the beach!

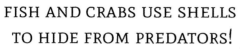

USES FOR SHELLS AROUND THE BEACH

FISH AND CRABS USE SHELLS
TO HIDE FROM PREDATORS!

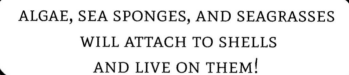

ALGAE, SEA SPONGES, AND SEAGRASSES
WILL ATTACH TO SHELLS
AND LIVE ON THEM!

AND HERMIT CRABS
LIVE IN THEM!

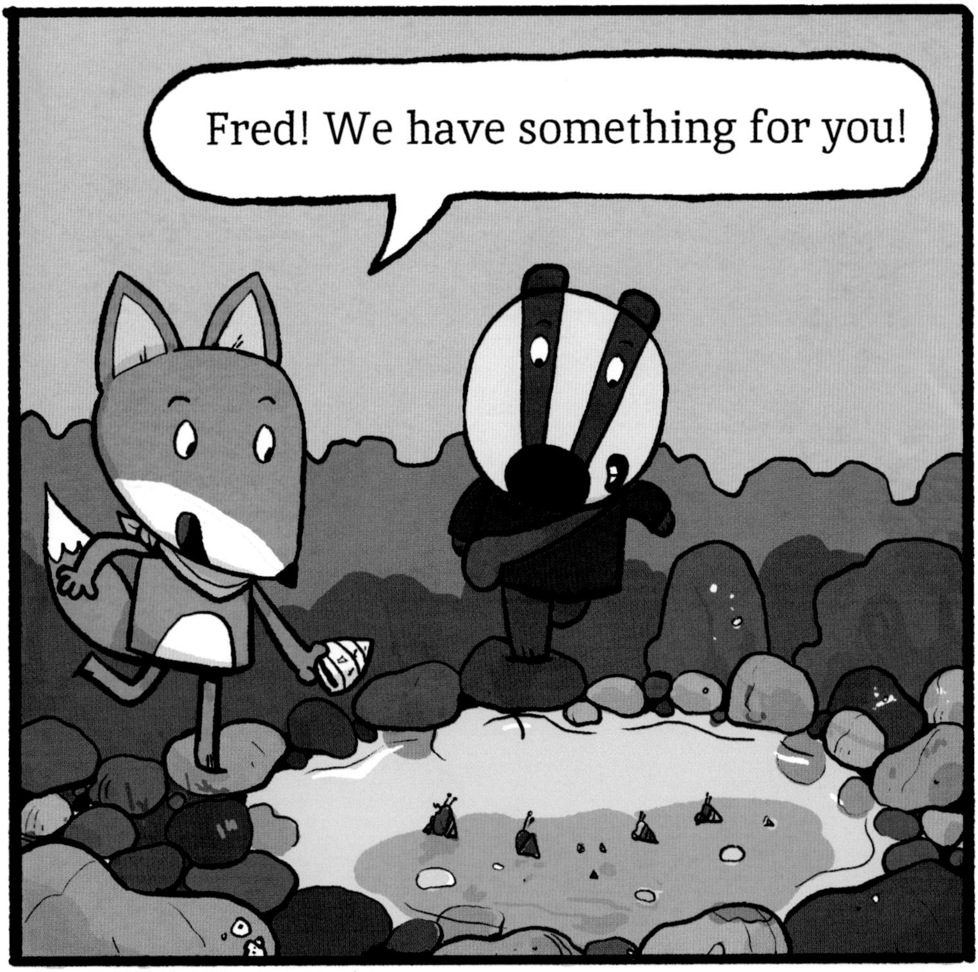
Fred! We have something for you!

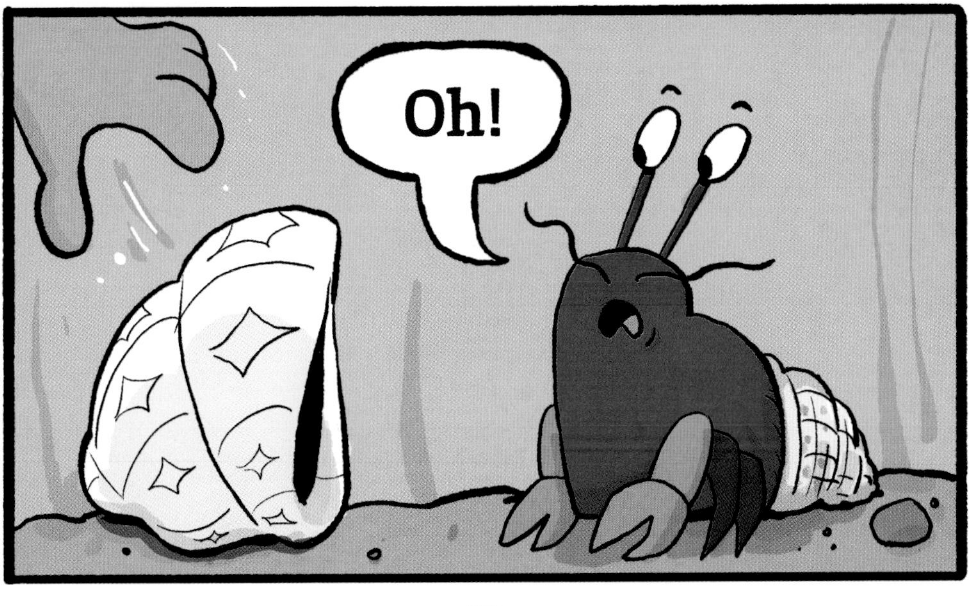
Oh!

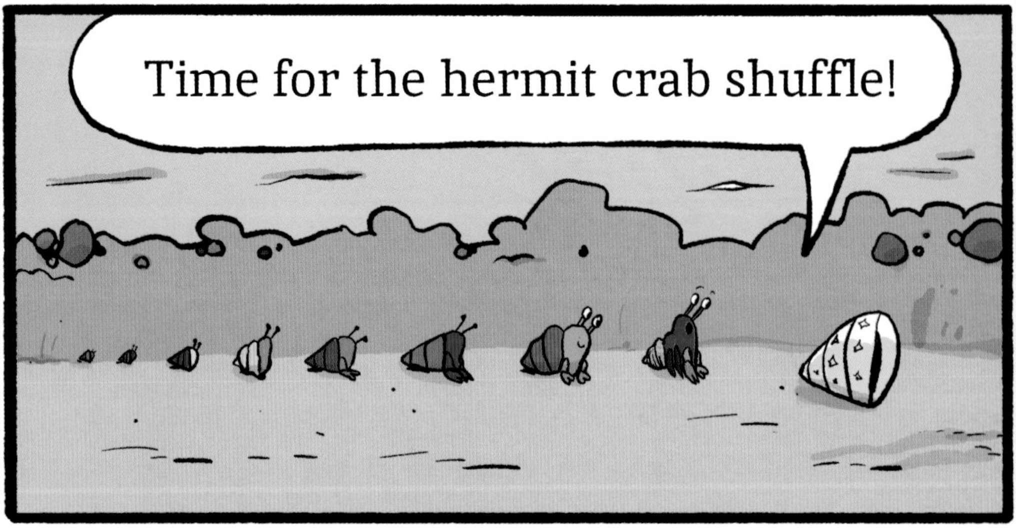
Time for the hermit crab shuffle!

THE SHUFFLE

AS HERMIT CRABS GROW, THEY NEED BIGGER SHELLS.

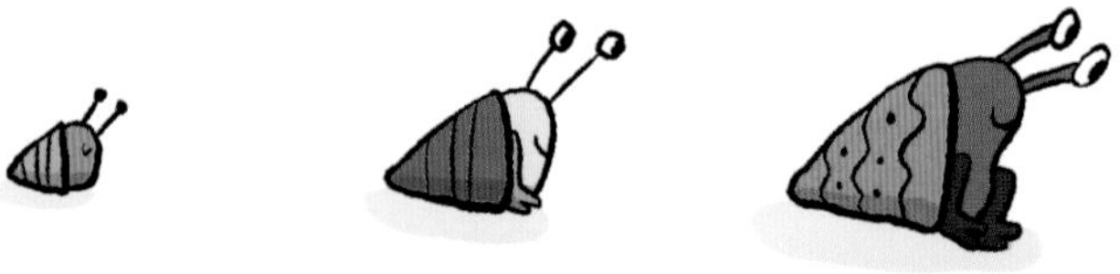

WHEN IT'S TIME TO MOVE INTO A LARGER SHELL. HERMIT CRABS LINE UP FROM LARGEST TO SMALLEST SO THAT THEY CAN TRADE UP!

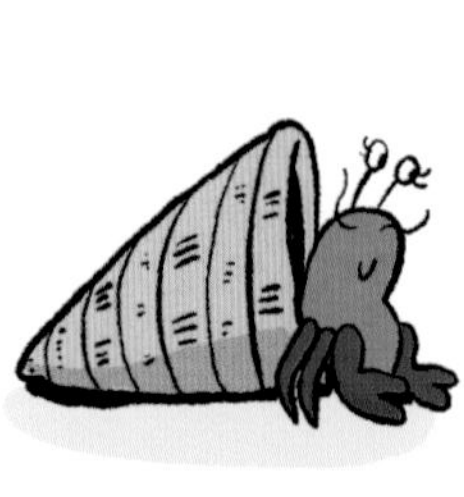

EACH CRAB GETS A NEW SHELL! NO WASTE, AND ROOM TO GROW!

THE BIGGEST SHELL GOES TO FRED, AND THEN FRED'S SHELL GOES TO THE NEXT-BIGGEST CRAB . . .

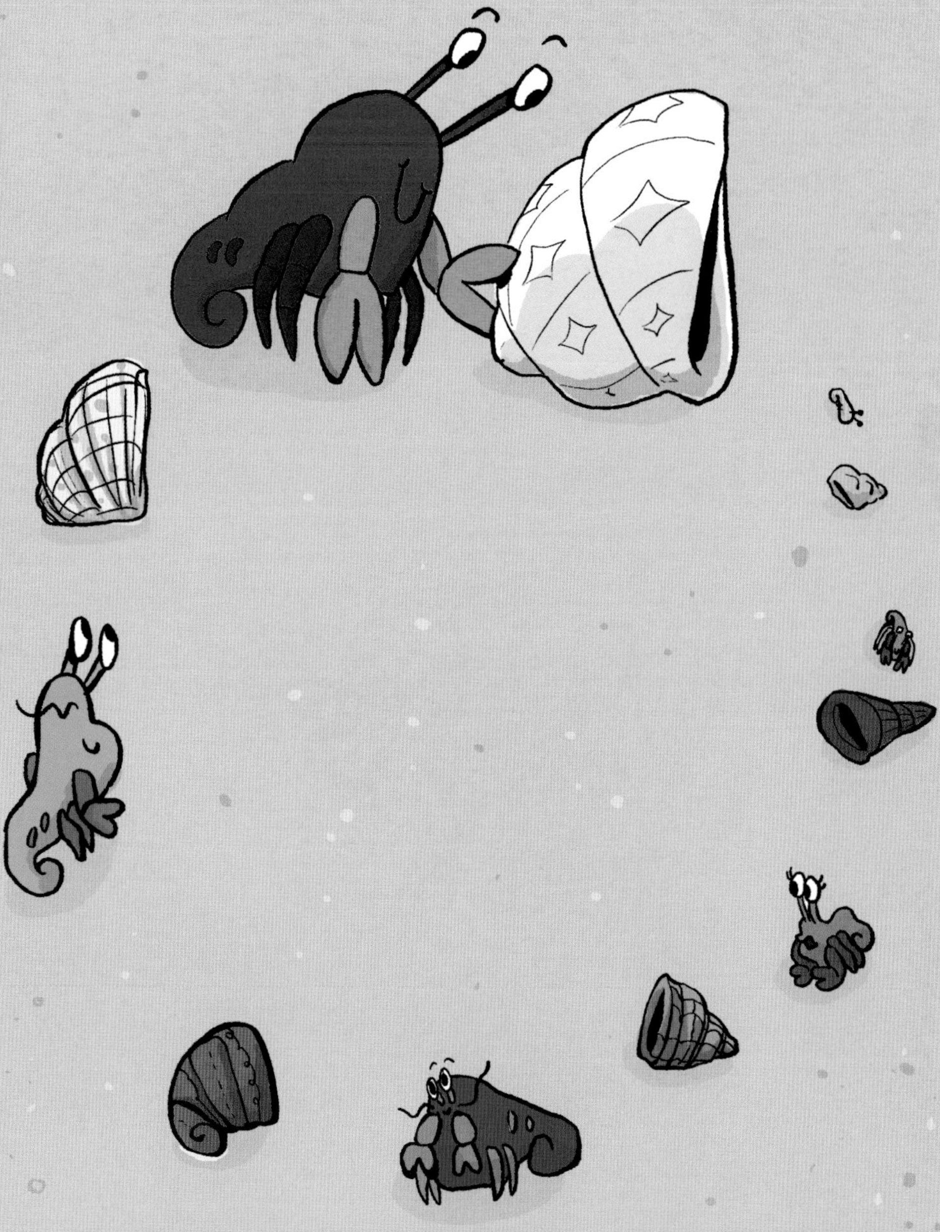

UNTIL FINALLY EVEN THE SMALLEST CRAB HAS A NEW SHELL TO GROW INTO.

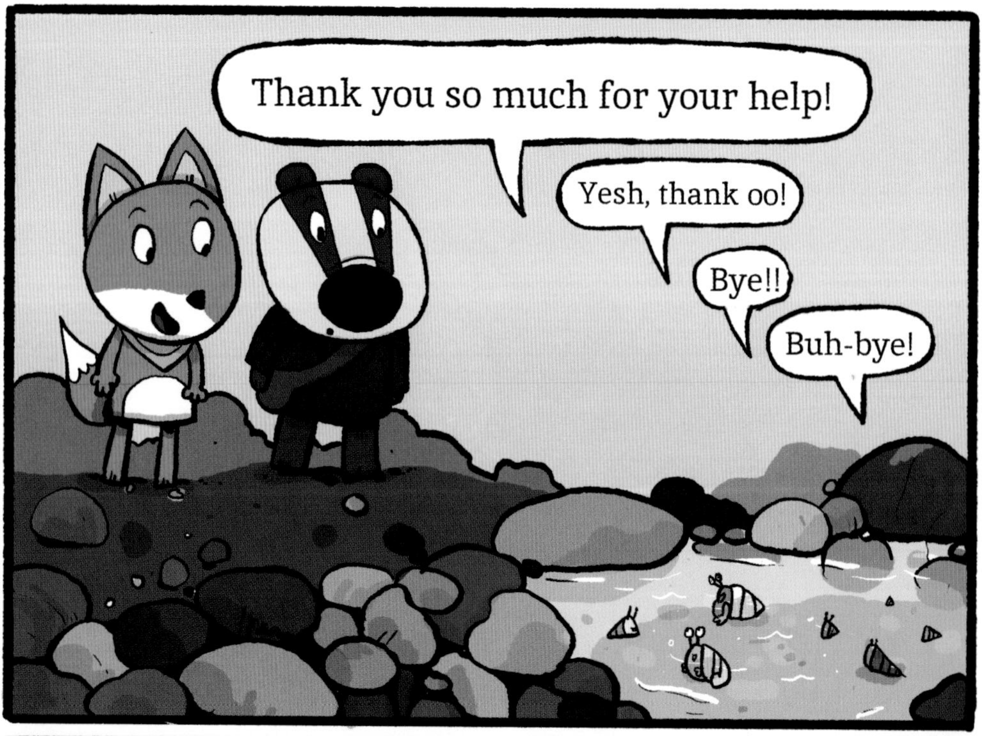
Thank you so much for your help!
Yesh, thank oo!
Bye!!
Buh-bye!

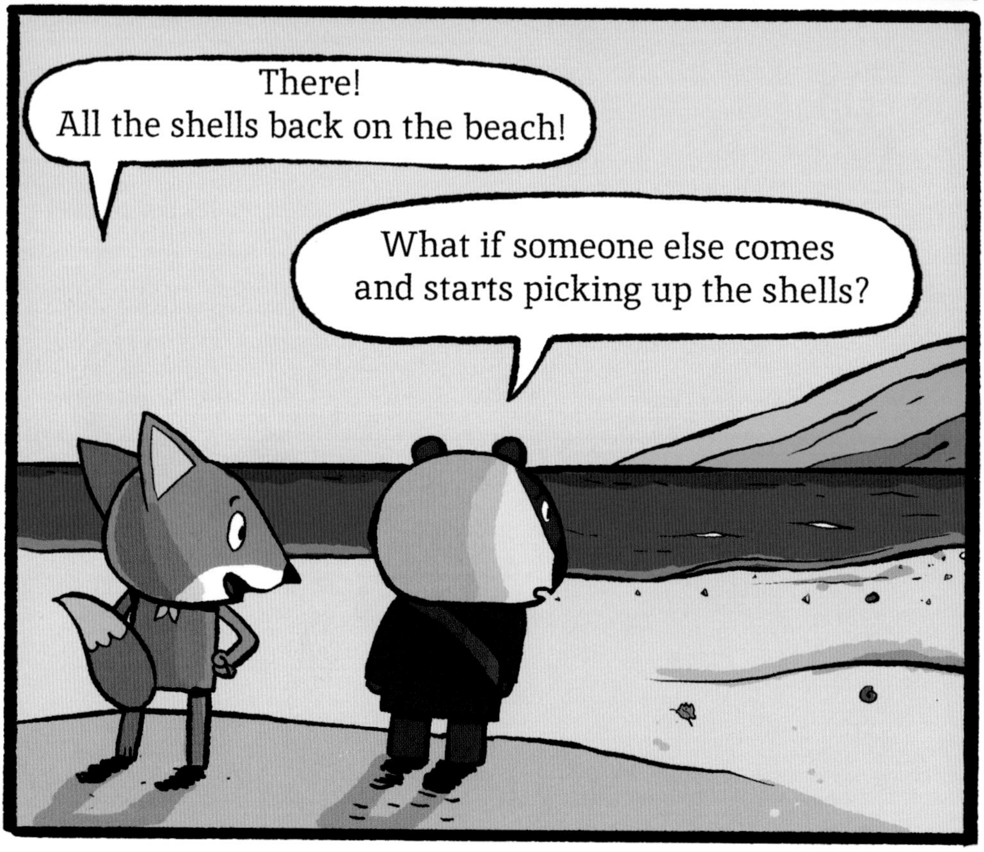
There!
All the shells back on the beach!
What if someone else comes
and starts picking up the shells?

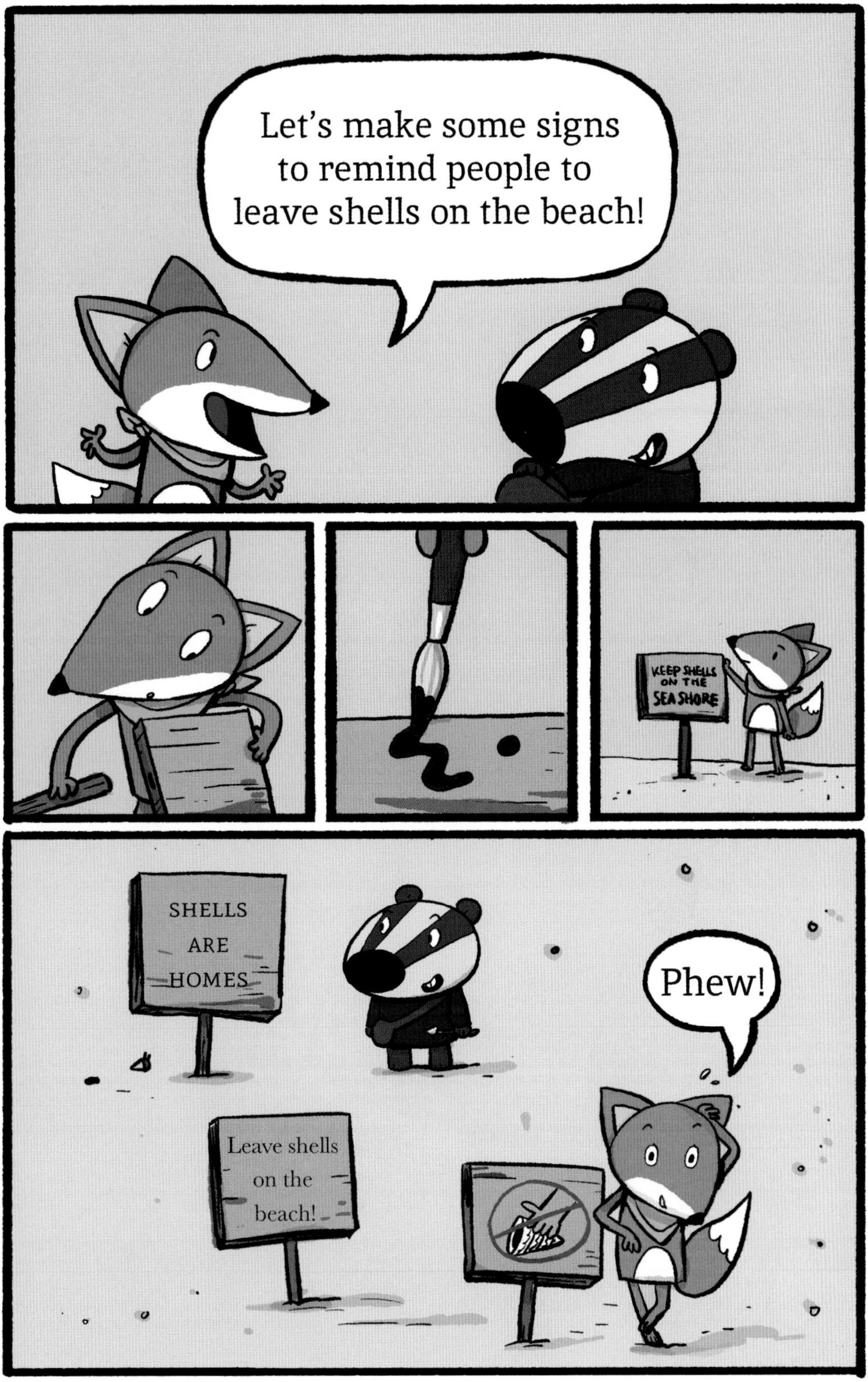
Let's make some signs to remind people to leave shells on the beach!
KEEP SHELLS ON THE SEASHORE
SHELLS ARE HOMES
Phew!
Leave shells on the beach!

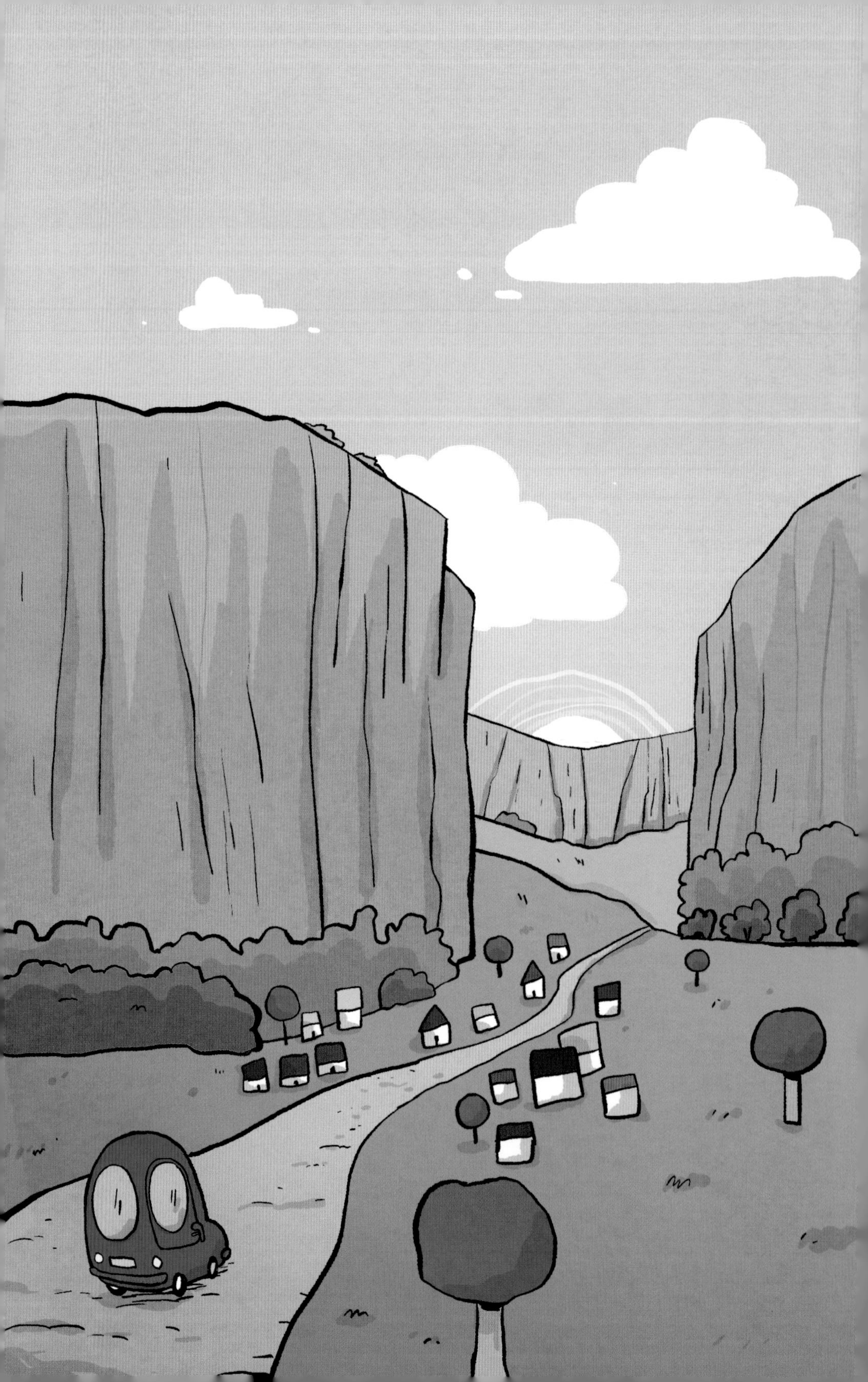

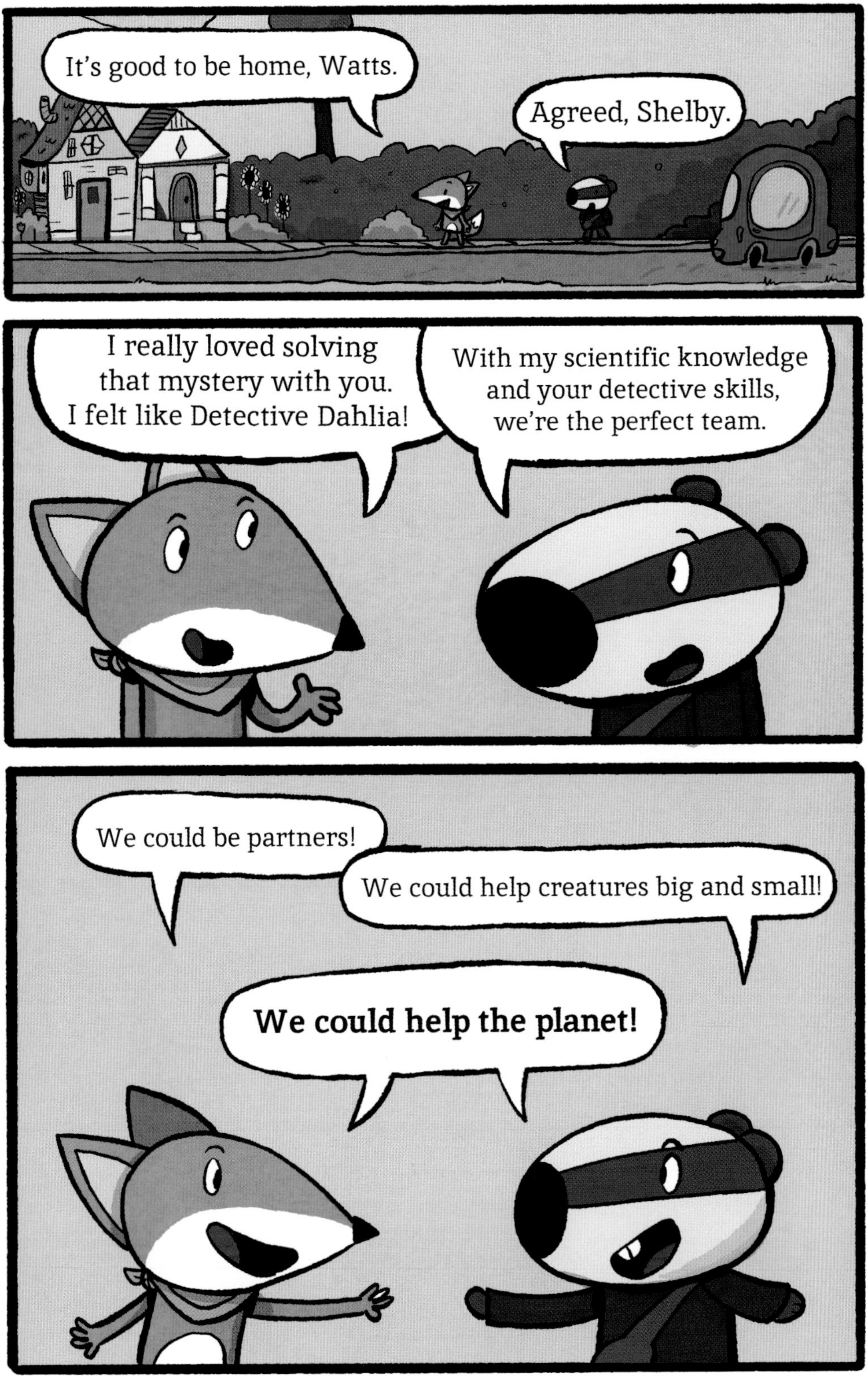
It's good to be home, Watts.
Agreed, Shelby.
I really loved solving that mystery with you. I felt like Detective Dahlia!
With my scientific knowledge and your detective skills, we're the perfect team.
We could be partners!
We could help creatures big and small!
We could help the planet!

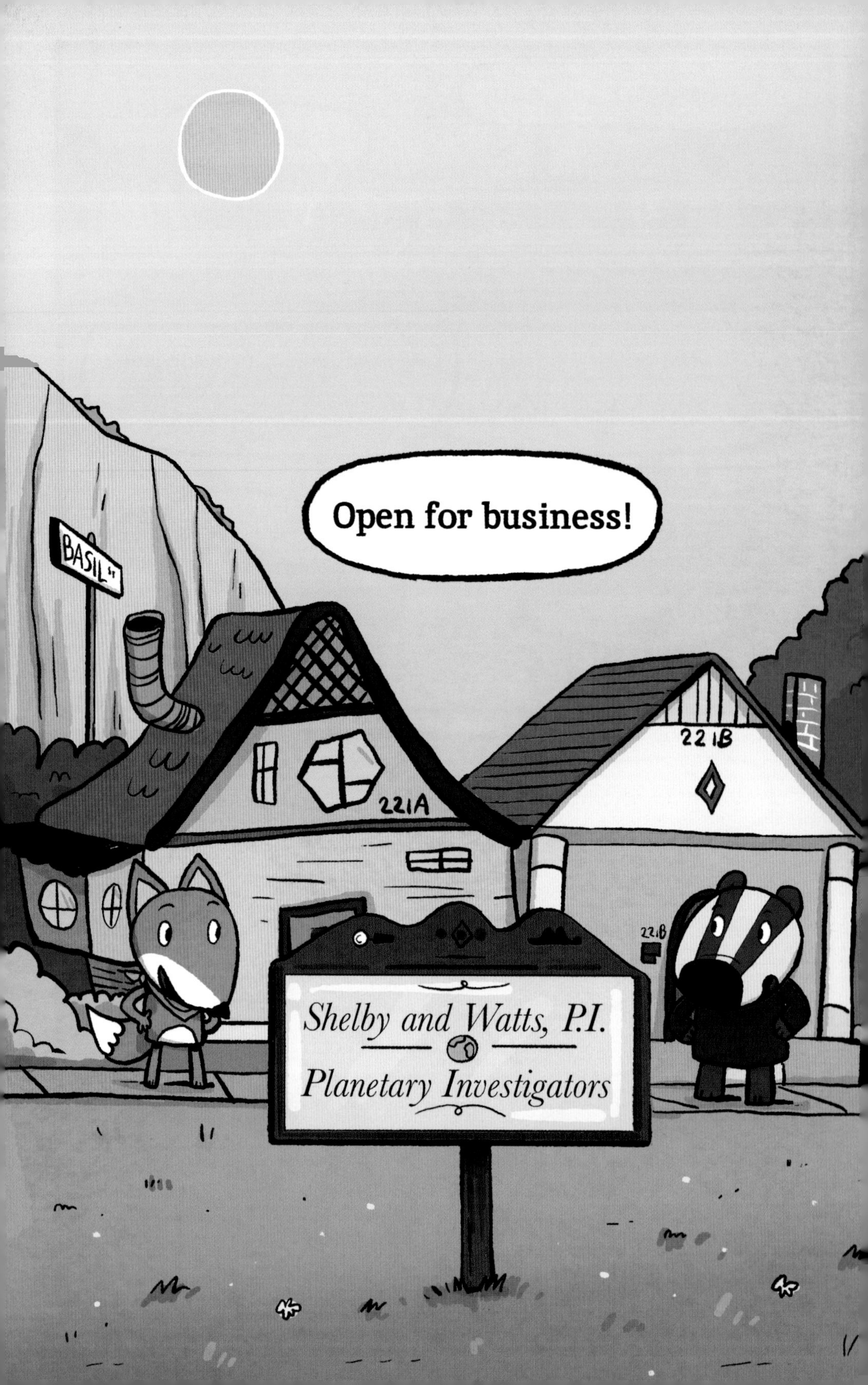
Open for business!
BASIL ST
221A
221B
221B
Shelby and Watts, P.I.
Planetary Investigators

Earth-Saving Tips from Shelby & Watts!

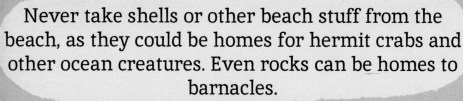

Never take shells or other beach stuff from the beach, as they could be homes for hermit crabs and other ocean creatures. Even rocks can be homes to barnacles.

Take photos instead!

Eat seafood from sustainable sources! This helps prevent overfishing and preserves our oceans' delicate balance.

Leave the beach cleaner than when you found it. Take all human trash with you, while leaving the beach debris (kelp, logs, and organic matter) there on the beach.

(A bucket can build a great sandcastle, and can also help you carry trash home!)

Organize a beach clean-up day!

We can help!

For Grant—my partner in all things

VIKING
An imprint of Penguin Random House LLC, New York

First published in the United States of America by Viking,
an imprint of Penguin Random House LLC, 2021

Viking & colophon are registered trademarks of Penguin Random House LLC.

Visit us online at penguinrandomhouse.com.

LIBRARY OF CONGRESS CATALOGING-IN-PUBLICATION DATA IS AVAILABLE.

Manufactured in China

ISBN 9780593205310

1 3 5 7 9 10 8 6 4 2

This book was drawn in Procreate and Photoshop on the iPad, with a few little
watercolor textures here and there.

Ashlyn Anstee grew up in a rainy city in Canada and then settled in a sunny city in the United States with her husband and four cats. She works in the animation industry, and in her spare time, drinks tea and takes naps. She writes, draws, illustrates, animates, and is the creator of the books *No, No, Gnome!*, *Are We There, Yeti?*, and *Hedgehog!*

Shelby & Watts: Tide Pool Troubles is her first graphic novel.